MARTIN CRUZ SMITH's novel about crime and politics in Russia, **GORKY PARK**, has topped the best seller list.

In **THE ANALOG BULLET** he explores the same setting of crime in high places, backstage machinations in government, and a terrifying conspiracy threatening the lives of anyone who got in the way.

Set in Washington, **THE ANALOG BULLET** takes you on a high-speed nonstop trip into the shadowy places and dangerous corners behind the bright lights of the political scene.

# THE
# ANALOG
# BULLET

Martin Cruz Smith

**Star**

**A STAR BOOK**
*published by*
the Paperback Division of
W.H. Allen & Co. Ltd.

A Star Book
Published in 1982
by the Paperback Division of
W. H. Allen & Co. Ltd
A Howard and Wyndham Company
44 Hill Street, London W1X 8LB

First published in the U.S.A. by Tower
Publications Inc.

Copyright © MCMLXXVII by Tower Publications, Inc.

Printed in U.S.A.

ISBN 0 352 310723

For
Sam Ervin,
Former Democratic Senator
from North Carolina

# INTRODUCTION

In 1970, Egyptian President Nasser dropped dead of a heart attack and Linus Pauling declared that Vitamin C could ward off the common cold. Joe Frazier was heavyweight champion of the world. The year's big book was Hemingway's *Islands in the Stream*. China was denied admission to the U.N. A Greenwich Village townhouse blew up and killed three Weathermen bomb-makers. After 300 years, the Royal Navy ceased its daily issue of grog. Detroit pitcher Denny McLain was suspended half the baseball season for talking to gamblers, and the rest of the season for carrying a gun. The National Guard fired on antiwar demonstrators at Kent State University. The big movie was *M.A.S.H.* Spiro Agnew was the third Most Admired American after Richard Nixon and Billy Graham, according to the Gallup Poll. And I was starting *The Analog Bullet*.

Not all these events were of equal stature. One I didn't mention was that a crusty, "good ol' boy" senator from South Carolina, Sam Ervin, had launched into a campaign against government surveillance of American citizens. This was two years before his prominence at the Watergate Hearings and Ervin was considered quixotic. So, I liked the man and I thought what he was talking about was important.

Governments always like to keep an eye on everything. The Soviets do, the Puritans did, the Greeks spied on Socrates and executed him. The difference now was that with the technology of computers our American government could—almost—watch everything. Data banks were kept by local police, state police, the FBI, Secret Service and CIA. The Department of Housing and Urban Development had a tape on everyone who applied for an FHA loan, and screened applicants through the Justice Department's tapes. The Internal Revenue Service started selling taxpaper tapes to the states in the '60s. Prosecuting attorneys routinely checked the tax returns of prospective jurors. The classic telegram was: "Flee-stop-All-is-known." All was known here and for sale, but there was no place to flee. 1970 was also the year the U.S. Army was charged with conducting illegal surveillance of prominent civilians. Henry Kissinger authorized covert funds to overthrow the legally elected government of Chile, and President Nixon decided to have secret tape machines installed in the oval office. Paranoia began at the top and filtered all the way down to struggling writers.

There is a time in a writer's life when he is trying to do two different things: write and survive. Surviving is like trying to tread water while holding a typewriter. This is both the most difficult and proudest period for a writer because he is desperately, ridiculously, supporting himself and learning how to write.

Some of the features of *Gorky Park* I can discern in *Analog,* although this is an experience much like looking at a high school picture of yourself. Look at that haircut! Those ears! After *Analog,* I became interested in American Gypsies, and Putnam's published my first hardback, but I still did a number of paperbacks from '70 to '77. They are the great training ground of American writers. Paperbacks are where you are forgiven, a luxury you only get in school. So it seems appropriate to me that all the royalties that come from this new edition of *Analog* should go to the Author's Guild and the PEN American Center's funds for writers in need.

Unlike "Smokin' Joe" and Spiro, but like the common cold, *The Analog Bullet* is still around. I'm more surprised than anyone else.

*Martin Cruz Smith*
*New York, July 1981*

The 7075 could retrieve 30,000 ten-digit words of information in 0.00000004 of a second from its data bank of magnetic tapes. In its steel-reinforced complex, the names and lives of 225 million Americans were printed on 17,000 reels to be read from the 234 computer units. Each unit was locked into the master computer and the master was locked into 100 more computer units around the country. Most of the outlying units were in military bases in their own graves with their own readers and guards. None of them had programmers; only the master had that.

The master had everything.

# INITIAL
# INSTRUCTIONS

MESSAGE: A8501-74-11-2-0314
ATT: 712USAFSKYSCANNERCONTROL
SUFFIX: IBM-606-8488553-4-DESMOINES50307
LANGUAGE: PLI
CODE: NEWMAN HOWARD
ADDRESS: 156302107712
INDEX: 5555555555555555555555555555555555555
                                                END

# CHAPTER ONE

Hank Newman slid down into the easy chair. The room was dark except for the television and everyone in it looked like a ghost. For the first time in four months, he let the smile on his face relax and disappear.

Damn, it hadn't been easy. The hand that held a weak vodka and tonic was raw and sore from shaking hands. His shoulders had been kneaded to dough by car dealers and insurance men. The muscles around his lips were stiff with the campaign grin his manager claimed was charismatic. His legs were those of a punchdrunk fighter from running through assembly lines and shopping centers and retirement homes, smiling understandingly and promising anything.

Just as long as they voted for him. As long as the calloused hands and feeble hands and hands with fake fingernails had pulled the lever that jerked an X beside Howard Newman, that was all that mattered.

"Shhhh," Jack Maggan said, unnecessarily, for no one was talking. He was the Newman campaign manager and he had the air of authority common to self-made millionaires.

The commercial was over. A newsman standing in front of an electronic tally board rolled onto the screen.

"Now for congressional returns across the state. The President himself put his prestige on the line against Senator Hansen. It is traditional for off-year elections

14

to go against the administration, the party in office, and the President wanted to beat that tradition. The Vice President made not one but two campaign stops in the state. But it appears, according to computer projections, that Senator Erskine Hansen is headed for his fourth term in the U.S. Senate and is even carrying a number of other lesser candidates with him."

Maggan's Irish face screwed up in anger. A few of the speechwriters sitting on the floor looked at each other nervously. One of them took a full bottle of bourbon from the table and filled his glass to the brim. It didn't look as if the free booze would be flowing for long. Nobody dared look at Hank.

Hank smiled. His lips made out "sonofabitch" silently. Hansen, that phony, fat-assed blowhard, the liberals' darling, had won again. But he had to hand it to Hansen; he was a hell of a campaigner to beat out the Vice President. Of course, his opponent was nothing but a small-town mortician. But, if the newscaster was right, Hank Newman was dead, too.

"The race with the most interest is in the 7th Congressional District, where Senator Hansen's protégé and former administrative assistant Ephram Porter was matched with a new face in state politics, Howard Newman. Nowhere else was there more contrast," the reporter went on for the camera. "Porter is a well-known, respected voice of moderation, a man with a professor's style. Newman is a brash lawyer, a hardline war hero with no political background who wasn't given a chance at the start of the campaign. That was before the disruption at the state college and Porter's defense of the students. Newman came down hard as a super-patriot, and the race has been rated even ever since. Tonight, Porter is awaiting the results at Hansen headquarters where the celebrating has already begun, while Newman is reported watching the election returns at the estate of his campaign manager, Jack Maggan. Very few of the returns have come in from the western part of the state, but we will be watching key precincts to find out who will be the next U.S. Congressman from that district."

The girls in the room, Maggan's so-called Newmanymphs, huddled in the corners. Their lipsticked mouths and red-white-and-blue miniskirts were frayed. An aide was in the next room on the phone, taking calls from ward chiefs. Speechwriters pushed the bourbon bottle back and forth like a pinball. Maggan came over and leaned on Hank's shoulder.

"It's not so bad. You notice the computer isn't calling it yet. The computer would've called it if things were bad. The longer it takes, the better chance you have."

"Before you said that the faster it calls it the better we are."

"Look, we'd be sitting pretty if you'd put that National Guard uniform on at the school. No, you were too proud. Big hero. We had the cameras ready, everything. That was 5,000 votes right there. Boy, I bet you'd put that uniform on now, wouldn't you?"

Hank looked up at Maggan's smooth, red face.

"Fuck off," he said softly.

The aide at the phone stuck his head into the television room.

"Hey, Ivans says there was some trouble with the machines, that's why everything's so slow. They should be coming in any second now."

Maggan looked steadily at Hank.

"Okay, Newman, okay," he whispered. "But after tonight you won't be a candidate anymore. You'll be a two-bit lawyer just like when I found you. You can stay home and count your medals. Because by tomorrow you'll be shit in this state, and that's a promise."

Hank swirled his glass, counting the circuits made by the lime wedge as Maggan moved away. He *had* been a mediocre lawyer, just as he'd been a mediocre law student. He would have gone into the Army for a career, but his father had been a professional soldier and said no offspring of his was going to make the same mistake. No, his boy was going to get rich off other folks; he was going to law school at the point of a bayonet. So, after football at Duke and graduate school at the University of Virginia on an Army Brat scholarship, Hank had become a lawyer. Not very good but smart enough to get by on court-martials while he paid back the Army with a three-year stint.

Second rate. That's what he should have put on his shingle when he went into civilian life. Specializing in divorces was how he met his wife, cross-filing for her on an adultery suit and then taking her to bed. She brought money and social standing and one or two odd appetites. When his reserve unit was activated for Vietnam, Hank didn't hesitate. He had been right, for the first time in his life he really enjoyed himself. He hung out with buddies in Special Forces, going on long-range reconnaissance missions during his leaves. A born hunter, he agreed with the war. If the Reds weren't stopped at the DMZ they'd soon be at the Mississippi. His first night back in the States, he took a peacenik out of a bar and broke his legs so he wouldn't march anymore.

The year after he came back was terribly boring. He got drunk, laid an occasional waitress, played a lot of golf and handled easy zoning cases. The only reason Maggan had asked him to run for the House of Representatives was that no one else wanted to get beaten by Porter. Hank had jumped at the chance; at least it would get him away from his desk. Now it looked as if he would be chained to his office. Ellie would enjoy that. She liked to see him straitjacketed.

"Hey, Irv, will you put some more vodka in this for me?"

17

One of the writers stirred from his position on the floor, a little more slowly than if Hank had looked like a winner. It was funny what subtle changes a few figures on a toteboard could make.

"Thanks, Irv."

"Sure, Hank, anytime."

On the screen was a report from Hansen headquarters at a hotel ballroom in Des Moines. Streamers hung from the walls there, and young campaign workers ran around excitedly with paper cups of ginger ale. A cheer went up as Senator Hansen entered the ballroom for his victory speech. Porter was at his side, beaming with anticipation.

In the middle of Hansen's victory speech, the cameras switched from the ballroom to the election returns center. A minute passed before one of the writers realized what was happening and turned the sound up. Suddenly the newscaster came through loud and clear.

" . . . so there it is. An astonishing victory for what was a few months back a political nobody. But with the reports back from bellwether precincts, the computer says there's no doubt about it. Howard Newman has defeated Ephram Porter handily. Not a landslide but with a projected fifty-eight percent of the vote, a definite mandate for conservatism and a surprising slap at another of tonight's victors, Senator Hansen."

Hank was stunned. He put the glass down on the rug before he dropped it. He hadn't realized until this moment that he'd adjusted to losing. Maggan had, too. He stood speechless in the middle of the room. The writers looked at each other in disbelief.

An older newscaster, an analyst, was on the screen with instant wisdom.

"Reasons for this upset are quite obvious. Porter was an old face with quiet, reasoned approaches to

18

social problems. Newman is a fresh face, a handsome, photogenic character, unafraid to voice simple solutions the voters could easily identify with. Moreover, he proved to be a political animal, a fighter with the killer instinct. It may be that Ephram Porter never had a chance against him."

Hank was standing up. He didn't know what to do. Maggan moved across the room, his hand out, an unembarrassed grin on his round face.

"Damn, Hank, we did it, we did it. Damn."

They shook hands and Maggan slapped him on the back. Campaign girls jumped in, kissing both men. Writers were on their feet, one pushing a glass into Hank's hand. The aide on the phone wasn't taking figures anymore, he was calling the Newman home to tell Ellie Newman, who was sitting as stiffly as a beautiful mummy in front of her television, that a car would be by to take her to the victory celebration at Newman headquarters in town.

"But it's not official yet, it's just a projection," Hank said.

"Relax," Maggan said. "The computer doesn't make mistakes."

# CHAPTER TWO

On a cold January afternoon, a farmer drove his pickup truck along the Potomac at Harpers Ferry. He was a worker on the farm of one of the Maryland Senators. The Senator had 4,000 acres of untilled land. His crop was in agricultural subsidies. Whatever was in surplus was what he didn't grow. This year it was sorghum, cotton and peanuts. It would have been simpler not to grow one product, but Congress had clamped down lately, and he could only receive $50,000 for not harvesting a crop. The Senator himself had voted for the reform. So he didn't grow three crops instead and took $50,000 for each of them.

The land didn't go entirely to waste, though. The Senator enjoyed raising prize cattle, and he had an Eisenhower Black Angus bull he was very proud of. The only trouble was that his growing herd produced a surplus of fertilizer. His farmer usually plowed in waste but now the earth was too cold.

The truck stopped and then went into reverse, backing up to the water. The farmer climbed out of the cab and hoisted himself up onto the pile of manure. He wore heavy fishing boots that reached to his waist. With two kicks he knocked the pins off the back panel. Then, in slow arcs, his shovel scooped up mounds of the aromatic mass and heaved them into the river. Each mound sank as it hit the icy water, then split into several parts and rose to the surface to begin its journey downstream.

The manure floated by the ferry that John Brown had once seized in hopes of revolution. Slowly dissipating, it traveled between Tuscarora on the left and Leesburg on the right, by now melded with industrial wastes and the sewage of suburban apartment complexes. The Capital Beltway passed overhead, scenting the scum with exhaust. The beaches in Arlington were studded with Contaminated Water notices. By the time the Tuscarora flowed by Washington National Airport, what the farmer had thrown into the Potomac had become part of the brown skin that covered the river and lapped at the yachts in the Washington Marina.

"Thank God you have this thing heated," General Weggoner said. "I'd hate to go swimming on a day like today. Freeze the balls off a brass monkey."

Mitchell Duggs, senior representative from Maryland, laughed. Ned Weggoner was next in line when the Army Chief of Staff stepped down. That was one reason to laugh. The other was pleasure in his own foresight for having the deck of his 60-foot yacht enclosed with insulated glass. There was no more popular party site in town than the *Onthaloosa*.

A black servant in a white jacket guided a bar on wheels past a group of women. The party extended the length of the ship, and in the evening dusk the *Onthaloosa* glowed like a yellow diamond as Congressmen and their wives squeezed sideways to pass each other drinks in the galley. For the invited incumbents the party was a return to the gracious pace of Washington life; to the freshmen it was their first taste of the glamor of power.

All the wives, whether they were from Manhattan or Davenport, Iowa, were dressed their best. Among them, Ellie Newman stood out, coasting through the crowd with her champagne glass held in front, her

21

pitch black hair and almost oriental eyes contrasting with her pure white Dior gown.

"Mrs. Newman, I'd like you to meet Ned Weggoner," Duggs said as he pulled her out of the crush. "I know he'd like to meet you."

Ellie smiled coolly, not over-flattered, and Duggs started putting the facts away on her. Fact number one was she was no hick.

"We've been looking forward to having you and your husband in Washington," Weggoner said. "Some outstanding record he had in the service."

"He enjoyed every minute of it," Ellie said.

"Here he is now," Duggs said as Hank came up, towed by the arm of Celia Manx, the Women's Page editor of the *Star*.

"This has to be the handsomest new couple in town. And I've been around since Hoover. You can choose which one," Celia said. "I predict a great future for this boy. Just as long as he doesn't lose his hair like the general."

"Hank, you know General Weggoner, don't you?" Duggs asked.

"I'm afraid not," Hank said. He had met his host only an hour before. "Most of the men I knew in Nam were sergeants trying to keep my nose clean."

"Well, now you're going to be keeping the Army's nose clean," Duggs said. "The service can use all the friends it can get in Congress right now."

"You can count on me."

"Thanks," Weggoner said. "I thought we could. You and your charming wife will have to visit Marsha and me at our place in Silver Springs. My wife is rather proud of some of the Japanese recipes she picked up during the Occupation. Hibachi cookouts, you know."

"Am I included?" a sonorous voice asked. Everyone turned to face Everett Hansen.

"You sure are," Weggoner said without losing a

22

beat. His tanned, rugged face beamed. "Just as long as you promise not to give any damn-the-Pentagon speeches in the backyard. Marsha wanted to go after you with a shish kebab spit after that last one."

"With Marsha's cooking my mouth will be too full to talk."

Amiability wasn't running high but neither was animosity. Everyone was too professional. Social talk eased the flow of business. Hank was learning quickly that power is a select club whose members follow the rules.

"This is the fellow I wanted to meet, though," Hansen said. Even on a conversational level his powerful voice boomed out from his Websteresque head with its silver forelock hanging down to thick eyebrows. Hansen's name had been entered at more than one Presidential Convention. If he'd come from a bigger state, he probably would have been President. "This is the fellow who dumped my friend Ephram. You ran a good race, Representative Newman."

"That's funny," Hank said, "I was going to say the same thing about you, Senator Hansen."

"You watch out for this man," Duggs told Hank. "He likes to get good, law-abiding representatives and turn them into rabid liberals."

Ellie laughed. It was a musical, secretive sound.

"Don't worry about Hank. When he says he'd like to drop every hippie on Hanoi from a thousand feet, he means it," she said.

"Odd things happen in Washington," Hansen said.

"Not that odd," Hank said.

An hour later, Hank was sitting in the engine room of the *Onthaloosa*. He had been through the whole yacht from the bridge to the staterooms, on a tour guided by Duggs. Hansen was no longer with them, but they had been joined by Cecil Ames of Florida

23

and Harmon Pew of Pennsylvania. Hank was not too drunk to know he was surrounded by three of the most powerful members of the House of Representatives.

"You should have seen them," Duggs said. "Ev gave him that old come-hither look and Hank turned him down flat. Polite but right."

Ames had a bottle of Johnny Walker between his knees that he poured from occasionally. His skin had a tanned leather look to it.

"I'm surprised," he said with pleasure. "Ev likes to make his converts, but I'm surprised he tried the charm on you, Hank. He should know better. Things must be tough for those northern liberals, they try raiding our ranks." Every "i" came out as an "ah."

"What we brought you down here for, Hank, is to tell you we've decided on a committee chair for you," Pew said. "As you know, a seat on a House committee is not given out lightly. Especially our party's seats. We're a minority in the House."

"And there are some liberals in the party, too, don't forget," Ames said.

"So even though we have the White House, there are actually very few members of the right stripe where we need them most in Congress," Pew went on. "Bright, new representatives like yourself are what we desperately need. Do you understand what I'm saying?"

"That's why I ran," Hank said.

"Exactly. So now here we are at the time when committee seats are distributed. You know what positions a freshman representative can expect, one of the last chairs on the Appropriations Committee. Appropriations is nothing to sneeze at, after all I'm the ranking Republican. But there are 51 representatives, 51, on that committee and you can just bet what kind of news a freshman can make, what influence he would have in a crowd like that.

"Or take Mitchell. He's our ranking member on the Foreign Affairs Committee. It's a very important committee, a lot of headlines, but a freshman would be number 37 on it. He wouldn't be able to get the microphone to yell 'Fire.' Of course, there are committees where you'd rank higher, like the Committee on Standards of Official Conduct, only twelve on that, but who gives a hoot about official conduct? Nobody would take you seriously."

"There's just one committee where a freshman has a chance. Internal Security," Duggs said. "Big name, confidant of the President himself, automatic return to the House by an impressed electorate, probably a boost to the Senate if he wanted that. The trouble is that freshmen never get on Internal Security; it's too popular."

"Then what do you have in mind?"

The three men smiled.

"Usually, a freshman doesn't get on Internal Security," Pew said. "This time we're making an exception. You're a decorated hero, a lawyer, a man who's not afraid to speak up against anarchy. Most important, you're a man we can rely on. When the House meets next week, your name will go up as one of the nine members of the committee."

For some reason, the three grinning men reminded Hank of the monkeys who saw no evil, heard no evil, spoke no evil. He too put on a properly pleased smile; he recognized the honor. Of 435 representatives, he had one of the choicest seats. This was no longer a case of being close to power; these men were asking him to take his share. It had been a fast three months since his surprise win over Porter.

"I'll try to justify your faith."

"I'm sure you will," Cecil Ames said, his leathery

25

face split by a fatherly smile. He poured out a congratulatory round.


"That's settled then," Duggs said.

At midnight, the *Onthaloosa's* gangplank hit the dock. The party was coming to an end; the number of high livers in the House is smaller than anyone suspects. Mitchell Duggs was on deck beside the gangplank saying good night to his guests. He held Ellie Newman's hand between both of his as he told her to be careful, Washington was a dangerous city.

"Where the hell did you sneak off to?" she asked Hank once they were in their car and headed back to the Watergate. "The whole boat was buzzing about you and Duggs and some other men going off to talk. What was going on?"

"Just welcoming me."

"Ha! I saw how they welcomed the others. A slap on the back and a kiss-off. What makes you special?"

He kept the car in the slow lane. He could already see the curved slabs of the Watergate far ahead. Not many representatives could afford to live there, but Ellie wouldn't have come to Washington otherwise.

"Why do you care?"

"Curiosity. Maybe I'm missing something. I'm just curious what makes them think you're different from any other piece of meat on the street."

"Everybody has to start somewhere."

"And you started by marrying me. So you owe everything to me. You don't have other delusions, do you?"

Because it was a night when he should have been proud of himself, Ellie didn't let up. Not when the garage attendant took their car, not when they got to their duplex apartment with its wall-to-wall carpets and optional Muzak.

"Look at him, the hero who went to war because he was afraid of his wife. So cool, just does his forty push-ups so he'll look sweet in his shorts."

She sat on the edge of their bed in short white lingerie, her elbow resting on her crossed knees. Her heavy breasts sagged over her flat stomach, their tips outlined against the satin. She smoked a cigaret nervously.

"Who's under you, honey? Anyone I know? Someone you did another divorce for? That's it, stick it in. Give her one for me."

Hank got off the floor. His chest and face were red, not just from the exercise. He was still in good shape. A mottling of scars and jumbled pigment covered one side of his chest.

"Come on, Ellie, knock it off. Let's go to bed."

"Perhaps to sleep? What else with a meatball like you?"

"Please, I'm beat. You win. Let's take it up tomorrow. It's just that I've really had it."

"You never had it. Believe me, I've been fucked by every bellboy in Washington already. Some of them I had to spoon in and they had it better than you—"

The slap resounded like vicious applause. Ellie sprawled over the sheet, her mouth still open, half her face crimson. Hank's hand tingled. He had slapped her before he thought about it, but then he was far more impetuous. That was how she always won.

The Newmans lived in a secret hell, and if there was any consolation for Hank, it was only in the privacy.

(excerpted from the)

# CONGRESSIONAL RECORD

Proceedings and Debates of the 94th Congress, First Session Vol. 120 Washington, Monday, February 3, 1975 No. 16

## HOUSE OF REPRESENTATIVES

The House met at 12 o'clock noon.

Rabbi Moishe Zlatkin Zeller, B'nai Jacob Synagogue, Westchester, Conn., offered the following prayer:

Eternal God, we ask Thy blessing today over this congregation of legislators. Grant them Your wisdom so that even as the hour grows darkest, Thy Truth will shine brighter than before. In a time of peril may Thy intercession bring us safely home. Amen.

---

### The Journal

The SPEAKER. The Chair has examined the journal of the last day's proceedings and announces to the House his approval thereof.

Without objection, the Journal stands approved.

There was no objection.

---

National Data Center

Mr. DUGGS. I have been advised by Chief Montgomery of the Capitol Police that the pipe bomb discovered in a men's room of the Supreme Court is on display in his office for Members who care to avail themselves of the opportunity. It is nothing new for Representatives and Senators to meet under the threat of physical violence. As long as we permit free access to government buildings, we will continue to place ourselves and the innocent constituent in the path of random, irresponsible, sick men. The least we can do is screen visitors who wish access to the public galleries and offices where potential troublemakers are now practically invited to create havoc,

Mr. FIEN. Everyone shares a common repugnance at the attempted or perhaps abandoned bomb attempt at the Supreme Court yesterday. The esteemed gentleman from Maryland is not alone. I would like to point out one or two things, however. The great majority of bombs seem to be left in washrooms. Should we have a screening process now before anyone is permitted to use these facilities? It strikes me that a wait in that situation could become hazardous in another way that perhaps the gentleman did not contemplate. Also, there is something plainly repugnant about the processes we have already instituted and that have been unmentioned, such as the searching and checking of all packages and the installation of ferrous metal detectors at the doors. I assume the gentleman is leading up to the subject of the national data center and possible employment of the information banks there to check out every American who wishes to see how his own government operates. May I remind the gentleman that what we have been discussing for the past week has been whether the data center should be dismantled. Not the million and one ways we can use this outlaw computer to force law and order on unsuspecting constituents.

29

Mr. DUGGS. If I may correct the gentleman from New York, the question is not whether the data center will be dismantled but whether it will be legalized.

Mr. FIEN. If it is not legalized, I don't see how there can be any more delay about dismantling it.

Mr. DOERR. I would like to know why the House of Representatives of the United States is equipped with only five display panels connected to the data center. When the bleeding hearts complained about phone tapping for the security of the nation, we were willing to create a computerized monitoring system for the telephone companies.

Mr. FIEN. If I may object.

Mr. DOERR. I have not yielded. To protect innocent citizens, we in Congress ordered the establishment at great cost of relays connected to the data center, relays designed to take voice graphs of phone users and instantaneously compare them with graphs of wanted criminals. No longer do we have thousands of men making thousands of recordings of innocent conversations for the purpose of capturing one desperado. The computer decides what conversations are worthy of concentration and, at the same time, safeguards the liberties of law-abiding Americans.

Mr. FIEN. If the gentleman will yield, I would like to note that this is a revisionist form of history. The monitoring of every phone call by every American everyday by computer or man does not strike me or other members who agree with me as an improvement over the eavesdropping on just thousands of Americans.

Mr. DOERR. Take away the voice graph and you take away the fingerprint. Both are recognized as evidence by courts of law. The great majority of Americans have been fingerprinted at one time or another. I have, for security clearance reasons, and I'm not

30

ashamed of it. What I am ashamed of is the fact that we are given only five display panels for communication with the data center in Monrovia while there are ten display panels for the Senate of the United States. Why should members have to wait in line to use a panel when one fifth as many in the Senate have twice as many panels? This is the sort of situation we should be remedying.

Mr. FIEN. What we should be remedying is the fact that Members and Senators are already using facilities of a center that is, in the opinion of the majority here, illegal.

Mr. NEWMAN. I can't help but point out to the Member that in his attack on the data center, he has practically monopolized one display panel for himself to elicit information to validate his attack. As best he can.

Mr. FIEN. I stand rebuked. (Comments deleted.)

Mr. DUGGS. Mr. Speaker, I ask that the visitors' gallery be reminded to refrain from applauding or making disturbances. We are all aware that the Member from New York also employs human beings on his staff, as we all do.

The SPEAKER. The gallery is so reminded.

Mr. DUGGS. I yield to the Member from Iowa.

Mr. NEWMAN. I thank the gentleman from Maryland. I would like to take this opportunity to cover some points that may be confusing the public. For instance, why we are debating a bill to legalize a data center that not only already exists but that both sides are using to substantiate their arguments. The fact is that the information itself comes from legal, strictly managed sources such as the Federal Bureau of Investigation, Selective Service and Military Intelligence and confidential Government offices like Internal Revenue and the Treasury Department. In other words, the information itself already has the force of legality. It is necessary data gathered for approved reasons, and it is withheld from anybody without a need to know, some of it, such as records of the Internal Revenue Service, available only on the order of the President. What we are now debating is not whether the information itself is legal—it is—but whether gathering it all in one place is somehow evil.

I'm not going to go so far as to imply evil motivations on the part of the bill's opponents. But foolishness, yes. The United States is now a nation of 225 million people. We are their representatives and it's our duty to serve this great nation as best we can. We are all sworn to do that, I'm sure we all want to. What are the worst problems facing the people who elected us? Inflation and crime.

The Federal Budget for 1975 is over $300 billion. That's about $3,500 a family. The budget supports the largest, least effective bureaucracy in the free world. But we can cut that budget and return almost $400 in taxed income to every family so that they can use it for shelter, education and savings. We can modernize our governmental bureaucracies to serve the people better and at the same time eliminate a waste of $50 billion that can go to solving the problems of the poor. We know how. The question is, why aren't we?

There are over 100 major governmental agencies now wasting billions of tax dollars and millions of man hours duplicating each other's work. The way they all amass their own records and revise them and lose them and re-amass them is not just legend, it's fact. What's worse is that you can multiply the confusion by fifty for state agencies duplicating the same effort. This tidal wave of bureaucratic waste threatens to either bankrupt us or drown us. How lucky we are at this point that American technology has devised the means to save us. How foolish we would be if we didn't use those means.

The problem of crime and civil disorder may just destroy us before, though, and free us. . . .

The SPEAKER. If there is another disturbance in the gallery, I will order the Sergeants At Arms to clear it.

Mr. NEWMAN. Local authorities admit they are powerless against the computerized strategies of organized crime and the hit-and-run tactics of drug pushers. We face an organized conspiracy to overthrow our form of government. We are in an unprecedented era of political violence, and assassins have already cost us too dearly. Let me remind those in the gallery who disagree that the Selective Service dossier on political malcontents was created only after and on the order of the Warren Commission; that the revamping of Army Intelligence tapes was done on Presidential directive only after the riots following the assassination of Martin Luther King; that Congress made the Army banks open to the Selective Service only after the murder of Robert Kennedy. Are we supposed to wait for another assassin to strike before we finally create an effective defense against this terrorism?

We should be proud that the computer complex at Monrovia has combined some of our law enforcement resources. We should put the rest of our resources on tap and make them available to any authority in the country with, I repeat with, a "need to know." At the same time we should conduct a far-reaching systems analysis of our Federal and state bureaucracies, streamlining them and pooling their data at Monrovia.

The Monrovia complex is one of the great technological feats in American history. Not to use the complex for the welfare, maybe the salvation, of America would be dereliction of our duty and oath as Members of the House.

# CHAPTER THREE

Weggoner had a hard, line-drive serve. The small black ball flattened itself against the back wall, and Hank caught it coming off, slamming it an inch above the telltale strip on the front wall. Weggoner had to crash into the wall of the squash court to return it, and Hank had an easy drop shot for service.

"Matchpoint," Hank said.

Weggoner grunted, balancing himself on the balls of his feet. Hank served an easy lob into the corner. Weggoner got the edge of his racket on it and sliced the ball off the front wall into the other corner. Hank was already there. He put his weight into his swing and drove it deep into Weggoner's corner. Weggoner returned with a backhand. The older man was still playing with strength but his finesse was gone. The ball bounced firmly into Hank's forehand. He caromed it deeper into Weggoner's corner. Weggoner knew what was coming next. He was standing flat-footed in the corner, his hand on the wall, when Hank lined a straight shot off the front to his own corner. There was no point in trying for it.

"Christ," Weggoner said in disgust.

"Good game," Hank said.

Weggoner rejoined with a more detailed expletive. He stopped and both he and Hank looked up when they heard clapping from the spectator's walk above the back wall. Through the glass they saw Celia Manx and a much younger, blond girl. By the time the two men picked up the ball and left the court, the women had walked down.

"Bravo, bravo, another *success fou* for the golden boy," Celia said.

"This is supposed to be a men's club, Celia. What are you doing here?" Weggoner asked.

"You wouldn't believe it, but sometimes even men make news. Actually, I'm tracking down Hank. I finally talked the city desk into doing a feature on him."

"Well, I haven't won a game in a month. He's all yours," Weggoner said. He draped a towel over his shoulders and left for the showers, not before giving the other girl a long look.

Hank could understand why. There were plenty of good-looking girls in Washington, most of them working as secretaries and hoping to land clever young aides. This one didn't have that available look, but she didn't need it. She was in an all black pantsuit, using it for contrast, the same way Ellie did, with her hair, almost white blond like new cornsilk. Her eyes were a dark, steady blue with long, practically invisible lashes. The smile on her mouth was ironic, a joke he didn't understand.

"Daisy wanted to meet you," Celia said. "Let's go somewhere comfortable to talk."

The three of them walked up the empty court bleachers and sat on the top row. A new match had started on the court below and they heard the erratic plop of the ball scuffing the walls.

"What kind of article?" Hank asked.

"Just what I said, our golden boy. Only two months in Congress and a seat on the best committee. Maiden speech denouncing subversives a great success. Most popular man in the Pentagon, man most in demand at Washington parties. What more could you ask for? I've never seen anyone make politics look so easy."

35

The girl called Daisy was on the other side of Celia. She leaned over and whispered into Celia's ear.

"Oh, yes, I almost forgot. Physical characteristics. Tall, dark wavy hair, romantic eyes. Good bone structure, strong chin. Wide shoulders, long legs, very athletic."

"Gasping for breath, a stitch in his side and a cramp in his leg," Hank added.

"Modest, too," Celia said. "You know what they call you? A cross between Cary Grant and Spiro Agnew."

"You mean I look like Spiro and have the politics of Grant? That doesn't sound like a compliment."

"You asked for it," Daisy told Celia.

"Yes, well, our friend here is not so easy to figure out as he first looks. Tell me, Hank, how do you explain your luck? It looks as if you lead a charmed life. The national committee acts as if you just appeared on Mount Sinai with a couple of tablets in your hands. Copies of your speech are going to Young Americans for Freedom, columnists are talking about your being the first of a wave of Viet vets in politics. Even that win over Porter was big."

"This is for the Women's Page?" Hank asked.

"Women think," Daisy said.

Hank licked his finger and scored one in the air for the girl.

"Seriously," Celia said. "Doesn't it sound almost too good to be true?"

Hank looked at the reporters, shrewd eyes hovering above bags of skin. In the pit of his stomach he began to get nervous.

"Seriously?"

"Seriously."

"I'll confess. It's because I have a good woman behind me, a loyal, unquestioning, unswerving wife who inspires my victories and salves my wounds."

The two women looked at him with blank eyes.

"I don't think you're going to get anything," the girl told Celia.

"But if you want to know the truth," Hank continued, "it's simple. I believe what I say. This country has let itself be led to the junkyard by selfish minorities and phony liberals. That was okay when they comprised a circus, but now they endanger the survival of the United States itself. I'm 100 percent sincere when I say that, and maybe lots of people like it. If they don't, tough."

"The Committee on Internal Security is more powerful than it has ever been. Some people say that the decisions it makes this session will determine whether the United States remains a democracy. Do you think with two months' experience you'll know what decisions to make?"

"I know what the average American wants," Hank said.

"You are serious," the girl said.

"Damn right."

"Oh." She seemed disappointed. After a couple of seconds, she excused herself and tripped down the bleacher stairs, leaving without a wave.

"You don't think the generals are pushing the committee to the political right, cashing in on the dissension over Vietnam?" Celia asked.

"I know it was the liberals who got us into that war."

He fended off her questions for another ten minutes until she gave up and asked a few desultory questions about his hobbies and what he enjoyed doing with his wife. At last, they got up and walked down the steps together.

"I have a question for you," he said.

"Shoot."

"Who was the girl?"

Celia smiled wickedly.

"Daisy Hansen, Senator Hansen's daughter. She came along to see if you were for real."

"Am I?"

The question caught Celia off guard.

"It scares me, but I think you just may be."

Weggoner was gone by the time Hank got to the locker room. He slouched down on the wooden bench in front of his locker and took out a cigaret. By the time the smoke got through gas traps, reactivated charcoal and celluloid, the tobacco tasted sour. He stubbed it out on the floor and still didn't bother to get dressed in his street clothes.

Celia Manx was nothing but a gossip columnist digging for something. She had heard strange rumors and thought they were news. The trouble was that the questions she'd asked were the same ones Hank had been asking himself for some time.

Why had he been chosen for the seat on the committee? He was not so egotistical as to think he was the logical choice; there were a hell of a lot smarter men of any political persuasion in the House. Why was a man like Weggoner taking time out to play squash with him? There were certainly more powerful legislators to woo. Why did Hank have time to play at all, when other freshman Congressmen were racing around town making waves?

That's what disturbed him. Things were just so easy. Pew had gotten him a press aide and the press aide did everything. Picked Hank up in the morning, gave him a few selected letters from the morning's mail and answered the rest himself with a good facsimile of Hank's signature. The press aide's own aides took care of the footwork of checking with the process of bills in various committees, handling constituents who came into Washington, sending back a regular newsletter timed for the deadline of the papers back home. Hank ate a leisurely lunch, and when the

House met at noon, the aide was there hobnobbing from desk to desk. When Hank gave a speech, such as the one on campus disorders, it was carefully, devastatingly complete. Whoever prepared it—Hank never saw his speeches until ten minutes before he gave them—had done an amazing job of research. The news that the student who organized protests at Michigan was the son of a former Red was front page. Not even the kid had suspected, his father had been so diligent in hiding his past.

No, it really looked as if Hank was Destiny's child. Some important people had taken an interest in him and were helping him along. He should have felt grateful and he did. But the more he thought about the helping hand, the less he liked it. He was going to find out who had written that speech for him.

The decision relieved his mind. He stripped and wound the towel around his waist. When he stepped into the shower room, it was empty. So was the locker room, unusual for this hour. He missed the joking among men.

The tiles were cold and wet. Water gathered in lumps on them. He hung the towel over the adjoining taps. He scratched his scrotum with one hand as he turned the water on with the other, first the hot and then the cold. It took some dialing before he got the right combination, steaming but not scalding. Condensation rose in a pillar from his body. He started lathering.

His hair was hanging over his eyes, dropping water, when another man walked in. The man was carrying a towel over one arm, but he was fully dressed. Hank wiped the hair out of his eyes and grinned. His poor press secretary, Jameson, had obviously been looking all over town for him.

"Have you got a message?" Hank yelled over the sound of the water.

"Yeah," the secretary said. He let his arm hang straight down. The towel fell to the floor, turning grey as it soaked up water. In the hand that had been covered by the towel was a .45. The press secretary pulled back the slide of the automatic, cocking it. He pointed it directly at Hank's stomach and fired.

Inside the steamy shower room the shot was an explosion; outside it was barely discernible.

# CHAPTER FOUR

The last four months were glimpsed. Death unfolded in the slow motion of a flower blooming.

As Arthur Jameson's hand buckled from the kick of the gun, a dull nose protruded from the barrel. The bullet separated and swam toward Hank. Its noise swelled and ebbed, lazily orchestrated. Hank dropped away from the line of fire, floating beside the bullet. It passed out of sight as his stomach began burning. Ceramic shards emerged from the black star in the tile wall behind him.

He bounced off his knees onto his elbows and his press secretary lowered the gun's muzzle to his face. Hank grabbed a trouser leg and pulled. A rubber heel rolled over his fingers while Jameson, fought to keep his balance. The secretary raised his arms as if diving, and the second shot went off, straight up into the ceiling. Hank pulled again and Jameson went down stiffly on his back. The crackling sound was his skull hitting the floor. The gun jumped from his hand and slid in elliptical revolutions to the opposite wall.

Both men crawled to the gun. Hank was in front. Jameson tried to hold him back but only scratched his back. Hank was halfway to the .45. It had rebounded a few feet from the wall, its barrel toward them. The more Jameson tried to hold him back, the harder Hank pushed him off so that they looked like a strange acrobatic team with a luckless act. Jameson let go Hank's waist and fell back to straddle his legs. Hank pulled his dead weight along over the floor. He was aware that his left leg was pinned to the tiles, but he didn't know why until it leapt spasmodically and went numb. By then the secretary was pinning down his right leg, exposing the taut tendons of the inside of the knee. Hank kicked back as hard as he could and moved another five inches nearer the gun. He stretched his body and his arm. His middle finger touched the barrel and knocked it two inches back. He touched the gun again and it shied away a second time. His leg was vulnerable but the blow came down too high, catching the thick back muscle of his thigh instead of the tendons. He heaved ahead and gathered the gun in his hand, the way a mother cat would snatch up a kitten, and twisted onto his back.

Jameson's timing was even better, more professional. Hank's hand was caught in mid-air, and there was a forearm across his throat. He had to admire the secretary's leverage. He couldn't move the gun an inch, but his head was being forced back until he could see nothing but Jameson's face and the ceiling. The forearm moved slowly over his protruding larynx and then he could feel the thumb and fingers searching for the carotid arteries. The secretary settled more comfortably on Hank's chest and leaned forward to put his weight into his work.

Hank had never noticed his secretary's eyes before. They were light brown with long lashes, and they were very patient. When he shot the gun twice into the ceiling, those eyes didn't even blink. The fingers slid under his jaw, massaging the hidden arteries. His left-handed punches flailed uselessly on Jameson's shoulder. The fingertips rested as gently and firmly as a surgeon's along his esophagus, not attempting to cut off his breath, just the blood to the brain. The strength in his right arm was fading and he would soon have to give up the gun. He let his head ease back and gazed at the ceiling. Points of vision winked like stars. The secretary leaned forward even more.

Hank's knee rose between Jameson's legs. The comfortable shift abruptly accelerated and by the time the secretary's head hit the wall it was traveling at the speed of a slow-moving car. Hank ordered the knee to hit again but he suspected it wasn't responding. It didn't matter because Jameson, rolled to the side. The doelike eyes were blurred and the last attachment between the men was the hand on Hank's wrist. Hank tried to pull away, but his arm was as weak as a baby's. He got to one knee at the same time Jameson did and they lurched into each other drunkenly. The secretary began swinging sloppily and finally hit Hank in the chest. Hank sagged against the wall and watched the gun drop from his hand and rattle to its owner.

Jameson, dropped over the gun protectively, feeling for the handle under his stomach. Hank told himself he should be doing something. It took all his concentration to get his knees under him; if anything, he seemed to be falling asleep. Jameson was on all fours when Hank landed on him in an effort so weak the man didn't even grunt. He hung on as the secretary teetered. First one knee betrayed Jameson and then the other. He bowed his head as his arms splayed out over the slippery surface and collapsed softly with Hank on top of him. As they hit the floor, Hank heard an explosion and felt Jameson's heart pound into him through the back of the jacket.

Jameson had no more surprises. In a few seconds his jacket began discoloring from the bottom up and the crosshatch of the tiles around him turned red. Hank sat and watched the red pattern move to the drain until he got his breath back. He crawled to the secretary and turned him over. He hoped it was a stomach wound, but the bullet had torn through the chest and heart and Jameson was dead. He was entirely limp except for the hand around the gun. Hank was reminded of a tail wagging a dog.

He got to his feet, wrapped a towel around his waist, and wiped the blood off his hands on the towel. His feet picked up blood and left pink prints over the floor until he washed them under a shower. He limped and had trouble swallowing but the most pain came from the charred flesh burn on his stomach. He felt no exhilaration from victory. The secretary's eyes were finally closed, ashamed of exposing the awful secret of his chest. He'd been the perfect press secretary and administrative assistant, Hank had thought, knowing more about Jameson as a person now that he was dead. Hank had killed men but they were smaller and a different color and it had been done in a group setting. He felt exhausted and at a loss.

He went through the shower door into the locker room. There were no members and no attendants, usually racing around with trolleys of laundry. That explained why no one had responded to the shots, but Hank couldn't think of any explanation for everyone's absence. He called out. No answer. He moved painfully to the house phone inside the attendants' station, dialed the lobby. After twenty rings he hung up.

He wandered back into the shower. Jameson was still there, like a permanent occupant. Possibly someone had paid Jameson for the murder attempt and the money was in his wallet but Hank couldn't manage the nerve to turn him over and take it out. In Jameson's inside jacket pocket he found no plane ticket, just a pair of glasses and a pen. He didn't remember Jameson ever having worn glasses, and when Hank looked through them there was no distortion. There was also a computer punch card, which might have been a telephone or an electric bill, devoid of identification. He laid the effects on Jameson's head because it was the only dry place, then he went out to his locker to dress. In his clothes, he walked slowly to the far end of the locker room where there was a bulletin board and a pay phone. Notices enjoined members to return empty soda bottles and invited them to join a Congressional basketball league. Hank called the desk again. He let it ring ten times and gave up, used the same dime to call the District of Columbia Police. His breathing was under control and he spoke calmly.

"I'd like to report a death at the Capital Club. A shooting."

"Go on."

"The dead man is Arthur Jameson. I can't seem to reach anyone else here and I don't want to leave the scene."

"Who is this talking?"

"This is Congressman Howard Newman. I think you better get someone here right away."

"Could you hold on for a second, please." There was a short pause. "There's a car on the way. You said that Congressman Newman is dead?"

"No, you misunderstood me. I am Congressman Newman. A man named Jameson is dead."

"How did Congressman Newman die?"

Hank looked at the telephone receiver. Could the connection be that bad? "I am not dead," he repeated. "Arthur Jameson is dead. He shot himself."

"He committed suicide?"

"No. It happened during a scuffle. I mean, he tried to kill me. Look, I'm in the shower room with the body. How long do you think it will take for your men to get here?"

"Right away. It's not every day that a Congressman is shot."

"Wait," Hank said but the line was dead. He hung up and walked back to the shower. Jameson hadn't left. The litter on his face looked irreverent and Hank picked it up. He couldn't put it back in Jameson's jacket because his clothes were sopping. After death the blood glistened with life. Hank tucked the effects

45

into his own jacket for the police. While he waited he smoked, leaning against a wall.

Two patrolmen, one white and one black, and a plainclothes detective arrived. The officer had a spanking neatness that reminded Hank of FBI agents. Hank met them at the bulletin board and directed them to the shower. The white patrolman took Jameson's wallet; otherwise, they left him alone. The plainclothes officer questioned Hank without taking notes.

"He attacked me while I was taking a shower," Hank said. He'd thought it all out beforehand. "He had an Army issue .45. He came up and shot and he missed. We fought on the floor over the gun after that and it ended up with me on him and him on the gun. He was trying to get up and I guess he shot himself accidentally. The main facts are that he attacked me and shot himself while doing so. I think there are some other people who ought to be notified, officer."

"You bet," the plainclothes man said. He was so cleanly shaven it looked as if he would never need to shave again. "You just killed a Congressman."

Hank blinked. A disorientation appeared to be setting in.

"Uh huh, that's Congressman Newman over there. And you don't have to tell me that it isn't suicide," the officer said as he looked around at the splintered tile. "A regular shootout."

"I didn't have a gun. Anyway," Hank said rapidly before he let the point go by, "I'm Congressman Newman. That's my press secretary, Arthur Jameson."

The officer's mouth widened without actually breaking into a grin. "You told the desk sergeant you killed Newman."

"No. That's some sort of confusion. Hey!"

Otto, the locker room attendant, had finally shown up. He was a thin man lost in a sweatshirt, escorted in by the white patrolman. The two of them stopped in front of the prone Jameson. Otto was very affected, almost in tears.

"Sonofabitch," he told the patrolmen, looking at each in turn. "I wished I'd been here. I wished I could get my hands on the guy who did this."

"Otto!"

Otto ignored Hank and went on swearing. "He was a fine man, Mr. Newman. Never seen him drunk, never complained."

"Otto, I'm over here." Hank tried to reach the attendant but the plainclothesman held his arm. 'Damn it, he knows who I am."

"Can you positively identify him?" the black patrolman asked. He took out a note pad.

"Oh, sure, that's what I said. He's Mr. Newman. Positively. I just wished I could get my hands on the bastard," Otto said and shook his head.

"He's crazy," Hank said. "Or lying. Let me make a phone call."

"You want a lawyer?"

"No. All I have to do is call the desk and one of the members can come down and identify me."

"The club's been closed since noon. For painting. There wouldn't be any members here. Don't you know that?" The plainclothesman was tolerant and amiable. His attitude irritated Hank all the more.

"Then what would Congressman Newman be doing down here?" he asked.

"Meeting you. Being followed by you. Or following you."

"For what reason?"

The officer's tolerance finally broke into a smirk. "That was between you two, I suppose. You say he attacked you while you were showering. I assume you don't take a shower in your clothes."

For a moment Hank thought of swinging. When he didn't, the man seemed disappointed.

"You're very smug and arrogant and you know damn well that I'm Congressman Newman. When I get someone down here to clear things up I'll get back to you," Hank said. He was sure the man was from the Bureau now. The agents operated with a free hand in the District. This was a typical case of bureaucratic conceit.

He was relieved to see General Weggoner stride into the shower. Weggoner was flushed and upset. As he should be, Hank thought. The Pentagon had no better friend in Congress than himself. Weggoner would be only too happy to resolve the confusion.

"I was just playing squash with him this morning," Weggoner said. "This is a terrible thing."

"Ned, thank God you're here," Hank said.

Weggoner brushed by Hank and went to the body. He was plainly distressed. A red line formed where his starched collar cut into his neck.

"Have you caught the man who did this?" he asked. His voice was thick with anxiety.

"Ned, tell them who I am."

"We're still looking for him," the plainclothesmen said. "The club was empty, as you know."

"Ned, I'm right here.

"Probably more than one of them," Weggoner said.

"You positively identify him, though."

"Of course. I just played squash with him a couple of hours ago. This is awful, an awful blow. He was so young."

Hank looked at Weggoner. He tried to see something different about him, suspecting that this was not the man he'd seen earlier in the day. Because the implication was clear: One of them had to be a fake. The trouble was that the harder he looked, the more he was convinced that Weggoner was real. There was even the slight bruise the general had picked up on his hand when he ran into Hank's racquet during the

48

game. By now, other men were entering the shower. Hank knew most of them. Not one acknowledged his presence.

The plainclothes officer pushed Hank to the rear end of the shower beside a door that led to the boilers. Dugg's press secretary identified the body as Hank's and then a House Office Building security officer Hank had never seen followed suit.

"They're all lying," Hank said. "What the hell is going on here?"

"They're identifying the body."

"You're sure it's not suicide? He's holding the gun," Duggs' press secretary said.

"We're pretty sure it was placed there," a new plainclothes officer said. "The signs of a struggle are plain. We'll look for bruises on the body, other fingerprints." A photographer's flash gun illuminated the shower.

"Come on," the officer with Hank said. He pushed him through the door into an area bound by the gray, padded bulks of boilers. Dry heat emanated from the boilers tickling Hank's nose, reminding him that he was not invisible, that he was alive despite the claims of the men in the shower. Another reminder was the gun in his back.

"Up against the wall. Hands up, spread the legs."

Hank tilted in spreadeagle on the wall. The agent must be crazy, he thought at first and then remembered that according to everyone else, he was the crazy one. In an insane way then he was reassured by the appearance of the second gun. Physical danger was familiar, something he could fight. The agent's hands slid over his chest and up and down his legs. He felt his wallet being removed and he heard it being searched. The wallet was put back.

"You're just getting yourself in deeper," Hank said to the wall.

"Sure. Turn around."

Hank let his weight go back on his feet and started turning. If the man was within three feet, the reach of his arm, Hank was sure he could disarm him. It was no good. The agent was six feet back, waiting for Hank to try for him.

"Make a break for it," the agent said.

"No thanks. You're not going to shoot me in the back trying to escape. All I have to do is walk out on the street. There are 434 other members of the House of Representatives and I know a lot of them and a lot of Senators and staff aides. It shouldn't take me long to find one. Then you'll have a lot of answering to do."

The agent's expression didn't indicate he expected that situation. The gun stayed pointed at Hank's belt. They heard the men in the shower leaving. Apparently, Jameson's body was being removed.

"It's pretty amazing that General Weggoner is a Red," Hank said casually.

The agent was amused. The sounds from the shower were gone. They were being left alone. For what? The stab about Weggoner hadn't worked. If not Red, Right Wing? Mafia? The only thing that seemed certain was that it turned on his being dead and that was why he was being left alone with the agent. He could cross the six feet before the agent could move his legs but not before he could twitch his finger. It was all time x speed = distance ÷ .38. The agent backed up another step, lengthening the distance that was too far for a poor lawyer. His throat was absolutely devoid of water, an empty tap. He saw the hammer of the gun strain back against its spring.

His arms were caught. The patrolmen had come from either side while he was concentrating on the agent. They drew his arms behind his back, the wrists up against the shoulder blades. The agent let the hammer ease back.

"I thought I was going to have to shoot him. You boys took your time," he said. It was the first sign of uneasiness Hank had seen in the agent.

"There was a crowd around the ambulance and reporters," the black patrolman said. When Hank moved, the patrolman yanked his wrist even higher until Hank thought his arm was coming out of its socket.

"Congressman Newman is dead. He was shot by a man who got away. We're after that man," the agent said, and it took Hank a while to understand that he was talking to him. "Newman was a veteran, a hero. We're not going to let some filthy story ruin him after he's dead. We'll chase you but if you're smart you'll get away. Stick around Washington and you're dead. Talk to anyone and you're dead. You've got a day to get out. After that, if we find you you'll wish to God you had never met Congressman Newman."

"I am Newman," Hank said.

He would have said more but the agent had turned his gun around in his hand, butt out, and he swung it with all his strength into Hank's face. The tip of the butt caught the bridge of Hank's nose, fracturing the thin sheath of bone. A wave of blood gushed out of Hank's nostrils and into his mouth. The gun came back on the same point from the same angle driving the broken nose into Hank's right cheek the way someone might jar a door loose with a chisel. When they were finished, one of the patrolmen gave Hank a towel from the locker room. They took him from a boiler room exit to an alley and put him in the backseat of a car. They kept driving until dark and let him out within a mile of Suitland over the Maryland border. By the time they were told to return and run him down, he had shuffled into the dark.

MESSAGE: Y77C4-75-3-12-1802
ATT: 202USAMILINTANNEX/301CHESNAVAL-
   ARMORY/302REHOCG/609DELDEFGROUP/
   215SOPHILANAVALBASE/717HARRISNATGD/
   304HUNTUSAMILINT/703CAPDEFUNIT
   OTHER: SECRETSERVICEHONEYWELL2300-
   9919/JUSTICEDEPIBM360-75-4007/
   FEDBUREAUINVESTRCA8-200-3659/
   USCUSTOMSRCA8-200-4203
SUFFIX: NONE
LANGUAGE: PLI/FORTRAN/COBOL
CODE: NEWMAN HOWARD
ADDRESS: 156302107202
RECODE: JAMESON ARTHUR
READDRESS: 194595411301
ACCESS: AMEREXPRESS5489008/DINERS73552A/
   HERTZ449702/UNITEDAIR64900/
   MASTERCHA2904493/MOBIL738475022
CORRECT: MOBIL73847502

                              ACKNOWLEDGE
NOTE: REALTIME LOSS 5539 MILISEC FOR
   ACK/THIS IS NOT A TEST
                    ACKNOWLEDGE RECEIVED
INDEX: 8888888888888888888888888888888888888888

# CHAPTER FIVE

He came out of the woods on a two-lane state high-way lined with spindly hickories leaving just a pale strip of sky. The air was cold, the end of winter. He chose the road north. It seemed darker.

Two miles up he found a service station. There was a light on inside and some men in hunting jackets were sitting over a counter. The walls were covered in a display of soft drink advertisements and posters. A selection of pecan candies resided in a glass case. The men didn't look as if they were in a hurry to move on.

"Holy hell, will you look at that," the first man said before Hank even got the door open.

He came in and leaned against the counter. There were three hunters and a man in mechanic's overalls, all in their fifties. Two had enamel American flags on their jacket lapels. The mechanic put his Coke bottle down hard and stared. The middle of Hank's face was nothing but a dark bruise. His nose was spread over one cheek. Both cheeks were round and blue. He looked out of slits and his upper lip was swollen; the center of his face looked like nothing less than a worn bulls eye. His shirt was brown and the grooves between his teeth were lined with blood.

One of the hunters got up and then the others stood, too, making room for Hank to sit down.

"Jesus, take it easy with him," the station owner said. "Can't you see the man's hurt?" All of them could see that but the owner was the host. The evening had moved to another level. Their rifles were in a corner under a water safety poster. The station seemed smaller and the night larger.

"Can you talk? What happened?" the owner said.

"Hippie," Hank said. He'd worked a story out but he was surprised to hear his voice. It was muffled, clotted. "He was hitching a ride, I picked him up. Hit me with a wrench, stole my car. That's all I know."

"Harry, you get the State Police on the phone. Don't you worry, mister. Cops'll be here in two seconds. We'll take care of that punk."

There was a phone on the wall. Hank watched the one called Harry go to it.

"Wait. You can't call them."

Harry put the receiver back. The four men watched Hank like a critical audience, shifting in their plaid jackets.

"Why not?" Harry asked.

"Could I have some cold water, please? I'd like to get this taste out of my mouth," Hank said. The appeal to hospitality put them off for a moment. The owner handed Hank a glass of ice-cold water. Hank swished it gingerly around his mouth and swallowed it.

"I can't let something like this get in the papers," Hank said. "My wife thinks I'm on the West Coast. You understand."

The men looked at each other, unsure. Hank was trying to pass off an awful beating. From his clothes he looked like an executive, though, and in the backwoods executives were regarded as strange creatures.

"What about your car?" the station owner asked.

"Rented. Nothing to worry about there," Hank said as confidently as he could. The blood in his stomach was making him nauseous.

"You got to see a doctor," Harry said.

"That's for sure," Hank said. "He won't talk, he's a friend." He looked at the men.

They had reached their decision. The owner was suddenly activated, reaching into the soda cooler and bringing out a block of ice. He smashed it with a hammer and wrapped the parts in a clean rag for Hank to hold to his face. Hank was genuinely thankful. His eyes were nearly closed up. The coolness soothed the taut darkness of his cheek.

"You can count on us," Harry said. "We're all married men. That's why we're here," he added with a laugh.

The atmosphere in the station eased into conspiracy. The day's shooting had been a bust. Hank shook hands with all of them and tried a grin.

"Where you from?" a heavy, bandoliered hunter called Tiny asked.

"Washington."

"Washington?" Tiny was excited. "You know what, I bet you ran into that killer. The one who shot that Senator."

"Congressman," Harry corrected. "It was a Congressman named Newman, Howard Newman. You didn't hear about it?" he asked Hank. "Look!"

He took a newspaper from inside his jacket and unfolded it on the counter. A Baltimore paper, the headline read CONGRESSMAN SLAIN IN CAPITAL. There was a photo of a body being lifted on a stretcher into an ambulance and also a picture of himself. Hank knew how bad the damage on his face was when he realized that none of the men saw a resemblance. Harry's stubby finger tapped the lead paragraph. The police, it said, were searching for a "hippie-type man seen leaving the club."

"See. Another hippie. Hopped up on LSD, I bet you," he said.

"Damn creeps," Tiny said in general agreement.

55

Hank almost fainted. He leaned on his arms, breathing through his mouth. The paper said that Congressman Newman, a decorated hero of the Vietnam War, before his death had been fighting for a national data bank on political protesters. The floor of the station was covered with old newspapers and magazines and Hank felt as if he were being buried by them.

"Hey, you better get that nose taken care of right away," the station owner said. "How much blood did you lose?"

"Look at his shirt, Earl. Can't you get him another one?"

"It's not clean, but at least it ain't bloody," the owner said to Hank.

"Sure."

The owner went into the stall that served as a men's room and came back with a faded blue work shirt. The newspaper had paralyzed Hank's nerves. He'd counted on a day's head start, that kept him going through the woods. Pain increased as the physical shock wore off; he became unnaturally aware of the blood that coated his mouth and throat and stomach. Earl shoved the shirt at him a second time.

"Go ahead. You can change in the john."

"Thanks." Hank took his wallet out of his back pocket and found the maneuver long and complicated. He pushed it onto the counter and headed for the stall. "Take whatever I owe you. No, I don't think it was the same hippie. My guy was bald as Tiny."

The stall had a door, he was thankful for that. The door enclosed the powerful, ammoniac stench, but it protected him from their eyes while he changed shirts. There was no way of explaining the uneven burn over his stomach. Besides, he didn't want them to see how weak he was. They'd call a doctor or the police despite his protests. His stomach turned in the effort of taking off one shirt and putting on another. He forced himself to swallow back the first convulsive tremor of vomit. He wanted to throw up the stagnant sourness in his guts, but he knew he wouldn't be able to breathe if he did. His nose was absolutely useless.

He buttoned up Earl's shirt, tight on him but better than the red rag he'd taken off. He would be happy to pay what the station owner wanted. From the wallet, Hank remembered, the wallet he'd left on the counter. With his identification in the little celluloid windows Rep. Howard Newman, the late Howard Newman. With all the credit cards to back up the identification, they'd probably called the police five minutes ago. There were no windows in the stall. He was trapped as completely as the smell. Sitting down on the wooden lid of the toilet for a minute, he hid his face in his hands. He wanted to cry but he was too tired. Finally he decided to give up and left the stall.

Tiny stood in the far corner holding a shotgun that looked like a popgun in his hands. The other men were on their stools watching Hank. Earl, the owner, hit his hand with Hank's wallet.

"Afraid your secret's out now," he said. He leaned over the counter and handed the wallet to Hank. "But you don't have to worry about us, Mr. Jameson."

Hank dumbly took back the wallet and flipped it open. ARTHUR JAMESON, 246 BALMORAL DR., SILVER SPRINGS, MD., it said. There were Jameson's credit cards inside and $45 in cash. The agent in the boiler room had switched wallets when he searched Hank.

"Nope, I didn't take a cent," Earl went on. "That hippie didn't leave you much. Me and the boys here wish we could do more."

Hank regained a weak smile.

"How about some food?" he asked.

Hank made himself eat a supper of 10-cent coffee

57

cakes and Coke. Earl and the hunters offered to give him a ride to Upper Marlboro. He took them up on it. When he had finished eating they gave him a chance to make one phone call. Understandingly, they went outside and left him alone.

Hank had the necessary change for Washington. He called the Watergate and reached the switchboard. The operator plugged him into his apartment and just as quickly pulled out the connection.

"Operator, what's going on?"

"I'm sorry, sir. I have a message for no calls to Mrs. Newman. She's leaving Washington tonight."

"I know," Hank said. "I'm calling about a change in the schedule."

"Then you want the chief of security. That's another number," the operator said.

"This is the chief of security, damn it."

He could hear the operator hesitating. Abruptly, he was put on HOLD and he knew she was talking to somebody.

"One second please," she said.

The phone rang in his apartment. He could visualize the confusion there, suitcases out, clothes on the bed. A maid answered the phone and said she would get Mrs. Newman. Hank waited, believing that the conspiracy was that of a few men and that it would take them some time to trace the call. He couldn't know that the call had automatically passed into the machinery of his enemy, from diode to transistor limited only by the speed of light. A new card was being punched out on him even as he spoke.

"Hello, who is this?" It was Ellie.

"It's me, Hank."

There was no response.

"I'm not dead," he said. "Believe me, somebody is trying to pull a fast one, but as soon as I get back, I'll get it straightened out."

"Who is this?" Ellie asked again.

"It's me, Hank."

"You don't sound like my husband."

"Because my nose is broken. I haven't got time to explain now, Ellie." Now that he listened, his voice didn't sound the same at all. "Just get Mitchell Duggs to look at that body they claim is me and have him call you before you go away."

"He already has," Ellie said. There was a drunken edge to her speech. "He's seen the body and he called me to give me his sympathy."

"Duggs did that? I don't believe it."

Ellie laughed. "Well, I don't believe you're my husband. I think you're some creep from a newspaper and I'm going to hang up."

"No, Ellie, don't! You have to help me fight them. They can't get away with this."

"Away with what? I don't know who the hell you are but I'll tell you this. Whoever killed Hank Newman did me the biggest favor I ever had. He's dead and that's fine with me and if you want to print that go right ahead, lover."

"You hated me that much?" Hank asked. The line was dead, Ellie had hung up before he'd spoken. He held the receiver in his hand and looked out the window. The men were standing around a panel truck and glancing occasionally into the station at him. He pretended to go on talking, acting like a baby with a play telephone because his mind had stopped, choked on facts that could not be right. He should have been able to call his wife and then she would have warned Representative Duggs, his friend, and the next day the whole mystery should have been cleared up. Instead, his friend was an accomplice and his wife wanted him dead. He added these to the other indigestible facts of Weggoner and the police in the boil-

59

er room. There was a very good possibility, he thought, that he really was Arthur Jameson.

He hung up the phone and as soon as he did it rang. Earl was behind the truck and it was unlikely he would get to the phone on time. Hank picked it up. It was for him.

"Hello, Mr. Newman, this is a friend. Please don't interrupt because I won't answer any questions. I just wanted to repeat some advice to you which you did not take the first time. You are a very fortunate man and I don't think you understand that. You are alive through, let us say, human error. You should take advantage of it and try to remain alive rather than get yourself killed. That's only logical." The voice became less officious and more confidential. "Do your very best to become silent and invisible. Work hard at it, please. As I understand it, nobody wants to kill you. There's nothing personal in this. Discretion is your best plan. If you persist in trying to contact people you know in Washington or if you even try to return to Iowa, you will be caught and we will take action. Forget about Howard Newman. What an unhappy life he led anyway. This is your chance to start fresh. Most men would give anything for your opportunity. Think of all the things you've wanted to do, the places you've wanted to go. 'Kennst du das Land, wo die.' Pardon me." The voice slipped from German to a wistful English accent. "'Know you the land where the lemon trees bloom? In the dark foliage the gold oranges glow; a soft wind hovers from the sky, the myrtle is still and the laurel stands tall—do you know it well? There, there I would go.' It's a pleasant thought, isn't it?" the voice asked, moving back to American flatness. "I hope you keep it constantly at the front of your mind. Howard Newman is now nothing but a mirage you're free of. Good-bye and good luck."

By this time, two Maryland State Police cars had pulled in front of the station. Their red lights rolled around in the dark. The first trooper inside the station found the telephone receiver hanging down beside the wall. There was no sign of anyone. The troopers split up and went into the woods with flashlights.

RUN

# CHAPTER SIX

The aluminum log cabin called Old Hickory was on an oval driveway around an empty swimming pool. Each cottage was designed in honor of a different President. A raised portrait in plastic of Andy Jackson hung over the bed. The man sprawled over it. *Old Hickory was not only a great General and President but a successful gambler at the races,* an accompanying biography said.

When Hank woke it was noon. The pain killers from the doctor had made him sleep longer than he wanted. He touched his face experimentally. It was numb. A bandage over his nose guarded it from his desire to see how straight it was. *Common men regarded him as their champion against the banks, although today he can be found on the $20 bill,* Hank read. There were twin sinks in the bathroom and courtesy cakes of soap in the shape of small white cannonballs. Hank shaved around the bandage.

The phone call to the station had been a mistake. It had reassured him when he was in doubt and he had caught on too fast that he was being stalled. Jameson's credit cards had been another mistake. Hank had been able to get clothes and a car with them. He had $300 cash from American Express. The face in the mirror didn't look too bad; most of the damage was covered by adhesive tape. He had Master Charge to thank for that. He went back to the bedroom and made the bed himself. Then he covered it with newspapers he'd picked up early in the morning, the *Star*, the *Post* and the *Daily News*.

... *Newman, a surprise selection for the Internal Security Committee, had led the fight in recent weeks for legalization of the National Data Center at Monrovia, Va. Since one reason for the Center is improved surveillance of potential political assassins, his death is bound to have an impact on the outcome of the legislative fight. In a reaction of shock and anger, many of Newman's colleagues are reported ready to switch sides in the impending vote....*

... *made a distinct impression on other Representatives during his shortened career in Washington. He was a hard-line hawk who denounced radical-liberals, hippies and anarchists. In just a day he has become a martyr ...*

*The President has demanded a full investigation by the Federal Bureau of Investigation....*

*The bill needs a two-thirds majority ... a coalition of well-known liberals and conservatives has demanded passage of what is becoming known as the Newman Bill ... no firm basis to the rumor that the assailant demanded sanctuary from the Egyptian mission ...*

*Refusal to deny or confirm reports that a man answering the description was seen at San Francisco International Airport....*

*Howard Newman was not what he seemed.*

Hank read the last story over. It was by Celia Manx. *Every report that reached this columnist described him as a reflex-action hawk, an arrogant witch hunter in the Joe McCarthy mold. I had only one short conversation with him which happened to be on the day he died. It wasn't that I found him a latent dove, far from it. But he struck me as a sincere man who was just unaware of political reality, a very average man whose record showed courage under fire*

*in Vietnam and remarkable talent as a vote-getter.*
*Washingtonians regarded him as a simple hardhat. I*
*had the feeling that under that hard hat lurked a*
*mind.*

Faint praise for an obituary, Hank thought. He
scanned the police reports. They came from all over
the country, wherever a hippie in a windbreaker was
seen. The FBI said it was putting their target on the
top of the Ten Most Wanted List, and it noted that he
could very well have cut his long hair. The physical
description was vague but, with the long hair cut, it fit
Hank pretty well. *The assailant overpowered Rep.*
*Newman in a vicious attack, Rep. Newman receiving*
*lacerations of the face, concussions on the top and*
*back of the head, contusion of the spinal cord of the*
*neck and the fatal bullet wound through the heart.*
*The Bureau believes it possible that the assailant him-*
*self suffered some wounds since traces of blood not*
*that of Rep. Newman were found leading away from*
*the shower. The assailant must be considered armed*
*and extremely dangerous, according to FBI bulletins.*

Hank took a piece of paper from the night table.
On it he made a list of the people he counted on.
Heading the list were Representatives: Ames and
Pew, then Fien from New York and Kinney from California because they were liberal enemies of Duggs.
The rest of the list was made up of other members of
the Internal Security Committee and his own office
staff and reporters. He tacked on Celia Manx at the
bottom. Inside the *Star,* he found a human interest
story, Cecil Ames and Harmon Pew a pair of gray
faces as they left a Bureau briefing. *Hank Newman's*
*bright future has been shattered by the last assassin,*
*if I have anything to say about it,"* Pew said ungram-
matically. They were with Mitchell Duggs and Ned
Weggoner. The story went on to say how Duggs had
decided to bury the hatchet with Fien and Kinney

until the murderer was caught and the Newman Bill passed. The Bureau had promised personal protection for Mrs. Newman. Hank was stunned when he read it. Not because he relied on Ellie any longer but because he didn't, and realization of the fact stunned him. Also, because it backed up what the voice on the phone had said about not trying to go home.

When he finished all the articles, there were no names left on the list but the reporters and Celia Manx. He added two more just to fill it out. Howard Newman and Arthur Jameson.

A metal Monticello was across the driveway. A family of tourists circled the pool in single file. There was a father, a mother and two small children. The children were too bundled in snowsuits to make out their sexes. A gust of wind made the log cabin's window shudder. The father looked at the colorless sky and blew into his hands, and the whole family turned back to their Monticello. It wasn't the season for tourists. The air had the stale chill of inside a refrigerator.

*Rep. Newman will be buried at Arlington National Cemetery with full military honors.* He was no hero. Competent, rather. He had the reactions of a soldier, and survival was the first reaction. He didn't overrate himself. That, he remembered his father saying long ago when they lived in a flat Army barracks in Kansas, was the first part of the battle: knowing what your resources were. His father resembled Andy Jackson, and Hank wished—the Kansas plain had been so devoid of irregularities they could see a jack rabbit moving half a mile away, and they would sit as still as two Indians waiting for the hare to come near their .22s—he was with his father now.

Duggs and anyone connected with him were out. So was his staff, chosen for him by Duggs. Jameson came from Duggs. The friendly liaison officers from the

Pentagon were out. That was Weggoner's end of it. He doubted if any other members of the House would vouch for his identity in his condition. Anyway, if Fien and Kinney were involved, it was impossible to guess who wouldn't be. The ideological mix was too complex. Right wing, left wing, moderate, hawk, dove. The labels didn't work.

It was getting dark already. There was no sunset, the day simply shifted to a sour yellow toward the scrub woods that surrounded the motel. He drew the blinds and turned on the television. He waited for the news through a children's cartoon he guessed they were watching in Monticello. NBC didn't disappoint him; he was their lead story dead and alive. There was a film clip of Ellie landing at home, a veil over her face. As for the fugitive, the announcer said, the police were circulating a fuller description. The screen showed an Identikit sketch. The long hair was gone and the sketch looked very close to Hank without being a portrait of Howard Newman. It was now believed, the announcer continued, that the man might have a broken nose since he was holding his hand to it when he left the club and since he was bleeding. The police were also searching for Arthur Jameson, Representative Newman's press secretary. Jameson was last seen driving a rented blue Ford. There was no official affirmation or denial to the story that the assailant had been reported still in the Washington, D.C., area.

In a way, the situation was good. They wouldn't have put the sketch on the air if they hadn't lost sight of him. He had more immediate problems, though. There were only three cottages with lights on: his, the manager's and Monticello. He couldn't recall whether the father had seen him at the window. Anyway, the blue Ford at the door was bad enough, and the manager had seen it and him. To end any doubt, the blinds at Monticello winked for an instant. Hank picked up his jacket. His suitcase was packed.

"What you are supposed to have over a jackrabbit is to know when to stop hopping around and go straight." Andy Jackson hadn't said that; his father had.

# CHAPTER SEVEN

Celia Manx lived in the National Monument called Georgetown. The one time Hank had been there before was in the daytime, and the narrow Colonial houses had reminded him of tea sandwiches set on their sides. At night, Washington's bedroom was different. The Potomac ran like a suggestive shadow alongside lawns lit brilliantly by floodlights to silhouette intruders. The crisp rhomboid outline of Hank's car, a Mustang now, stopped on the river side of the street. He waited for a moment, the engine in neutral, then he turned it off and got out.

He didn't look out of place, except for the lack of a briefcase. Most government officials had hats and mufflers, but he walked as far away from streetlamps as he could. Georgetown had one of the highest burglary rates in the nation, and patrol cars cruised a street every five minutes. Celia Manx lived on the other side of the block. He controlled the urge to run, but he was happy when he could leave the street for the foyer of her townhouse.

There were only two names and two mailboxes. He leaned on the button under MANX. He had a story ready about coming from Duggs, but suddenly Celia Manx's voice came through the grill of the intercom telling him to come right up. He looked around the foyer. There was no camera. She was expecting somebody.

He went up to the second floor, where the wallpaper shifted from dogwood to red velvet. Gaudy was her style, he recalled. The door was solid and it had a peephole. Celia didn't use it, and when she tried to shut the door, Hank was halfway through. He pushed it open the rest of the way and locked it behind him.

Celia Manx was in a pajama suit. Oversized pearl earrings bounced off her shoulders as she looked Hank up and down.

"Is this a mugging or a rape or both? You'll have to make it quick because people are coming."

"Neither." His voice still sounded like a croak.

"Well, you better make up your mind, Batman, because otherwise I scream."

Hank pulled the scarf off his face. Celia found herself looking at a big man with the middle of his face covered with white. His eyes looked at her through purple lids and his lips were puffy and raw. Celia found a scream, a real scream, dying in her throat.

"I'm Howard Newman," Hank said.

Celia stared at him, at the patchwork of his face.

"You talked to me two days ago," Hank said. "I'm alive."

"What do you want?" What Hank said meant nothing to her.

"I'm telling you that I'm not dead. There's some sort of plot."

Celia shook her head. "I don't know who you are. Howard Newman is dead. They're burying him this week."

"Look at me."

Celia turned her head. When she got up the nerve, she looked again at the border of the damage.

"I was playing squash with General Weggoner and then you and I talked."

"Your voice is different."

"You'd sound different too if someone broke your nose."

70

Celia blinked. "You're the man they're looking for."

"That's right. To make sure I'm really dead. We sat on the bleachers, in the back row."

"What did we talk about?"

"You wanted something about Congress's handsomest couple."

Celia thought of the description of the dead man's wounds. She took a step back. Hank smiled painfully.

"I don't have a gun. But Jameson did. He's the one they found in the shower. I killed him in self-defense."

Celia's legs bumped into a low sofa and she sat down. Hank looked around. The apartment's decor was something between Danish and Japanese. The wall had silk screens and plaques and dozens of photos.

"You want another prize, Miss Manx? Help me stop them."

"Them? Who's them?"

"I don't know. But Duggs is with them and so is Weggoner and Ames and Pew. Maybe Fien and Kinney. And someone in the FBI."

"Why not pick the President, too?" Celia asked with a shrill laugh. "You've got everyone else."

"You recognize me."

"No. No, damn it, I don't. I only met you . . . Representative Newman once. How can I tell who you are with that thing on?"

"Do you want me to take it off?"

"No," Celia said after the time it took for her heart to beat again. "Keep it on." Her hands fumbled over the top of a lacquered box and took out a cigarette. She offered him one and he shook his head.

"Sorry," she said. "That was stupid." She lit one up for herself and dragged on it deeply. "Sit down, please."

"A girl was with you. Senator Hansen's daughter."

71

Hank sat down on the other side of a coffee table. There was a resemblance, she decided. She had met the man someplace before. In any case, he was right. This was a story.

"That's right. You two hit it off pretty well."

"The hell we did. She got insulted and left."

"Maybe you are Howard Newman. What do you want me to do? How can I help you?"

"You can call people. You can find out whether they're involved with Duggs. Ask them whether or not they've seen the body. Find out who the FBI man at the club was. Who Jameson worked for before me and Duggs. When you get someone who sounds skeptical, ask if they remember me well enough to recognize me."

"Don't you know who to call?"

"All the ones I would have called are with them. Besides, you're a reporter. You can ask all these questions. And you know people at the White House I never heard of. Believe me, we can break the whole thing easily once we get started. We've just got to get somewhere before the police pick me up."

"The cops wouldn't—"

"The District Police would do anything they're told to. You know that. They're anxious. They have to get me before I look like myself again."

"When do you want to start?" Celia's attitude had changed to efficiency. The man was probably mad as a hatter, she thought, but he was involved in the assassination somehow. At the very least, he looked like he should be humored. She was more than an ordinary gossip columnist and she wanted whatever story there was.

"Now. I have a car down the street. I stole it an hour ago and the police are looking for it by now."

"Okay." She got up and went to her desk. Keeping an eye on her guest, she grabbed the phone and a worn leather address book. Celia flipped through it. "This is a good one. Assistant Secretary at the Justice Department, Criminal Division. He's always had an honest streak."

Hank felt his muscles relaxing. Celia Manx looked as tough as a bulldog in her garish pajama suit. He felt he'd chosen a good ally. When she said it would take a while to get her man on the phone and suggested that he get a bite to eat from the kitchen, Hank took her up on it. She was still waiting, pencil in hand, when he came back with a beer and a cold chicken leg.

"Hello, Al? This is Celia Manx. . . . I have better things to do than make sure you get to bed early. You have a wife for that. . . . No, not just to insult you. Have you got a couple of minutes to talk? . . . About Newman. Who's handling it, anyway, you or the Bureau? Reports are very vague on that. . . . A commission? What kind of police procedure is that? . . . You're on it? Have you seen Newman's body then? . . . Why not? . . . Just curious. One other thing. Has anybody seen the body and said it wasn't Newman? . . . Just asking questions, Al, but maybe I do. Let me ask one more. . . . Just one. Are you perfectly satisfied with the way the investigation has been handled? . . . You don't sound very positive. . . . I'm not suggesting anything, but I might in a while. You sound interested. . . . I will, promise. Good night."

She hung up and looked at Hank with a frown. "They've formed a commission to oversee the investigation. Duggs is head of it. Al didn't sound too happy at all."

Hank found himself smiling. The opposition hadn't been prepared for a counterattack. Celia opened her book to another page. "This is about the only bastard I'd trust with my purse in the whole Bureau, and he just happens to be on the commission, too. I want to find out if AI's just griping about the Bureau as usual."

She got an immediate answer this time. Without missing a beat, she slipped into the same banter of the first call. Hank only half-listened as he pulled the chicken into small enough bits to put in his mouth. The beer was tasteless, but sharp and cold. Then he heard Celia getting to the point.

"Why don't they just let you handle it? After all, you boys are supposed to be the investigative agency. . . . Bull. I hear you had a man down in the shower ten minutes after Newman was shot. . . . From a very good source. What are you complaining about? It shows how on the ball you are. . . . Would you swear to that? No reason to lie, you can just deny it later. . . . Okay, okay, you didn't. By the way, have you seen the body? I guess you must have since the Bureau did the autopsy. . . . What's the secret about that? Did you or didn't you do the autopsy? . . . No, I'm not a crime reporter but I can just call up a crime reporter and have him ask you. I thought you'd rather talk to a friend. . . . Then I want you to deny it. . . . Then who is in charge? . . ."

Celia winced and put the receiver down gently.

"He hung up."

"What did he say?"

She put the pencil on its end and let her stubby fingers slide down it. She was looking at Hank harder.

"There's something fishy here, all right. George wouldn't give me a straight answer on the autopsy. I could hear his guts coming out. The Bureau has the best forensic lab in the country, and, you know, he wanted to say that the body went where it should have. And he absolutely denies there was an agent down in the shower until an hour later when the President called them in."

"Did he see the body?"

"Yes, he did. So far as he knows it's Howard Newman."

"Did he say who was in charge?"

"That was when he hung up, the sonofabitch."

She was coming over to his side. Hank knew it. He finished the rest of the beer, letting his back settle into the sofa's curve.

"You know, I'm beginning to—"

She stopped in mid-sentence. The phone was ringing, demanding to be picked up. Celia raised her gray eyebrows.

"Maybe it's Al again."

It wasn't Al. Hank knew it from the second she began listening. Her expression was blank, the face for a stranger. "But—" she said, just once. There was no banter. Then her face began changing, becoming red and malleable as if it were a rubber mask deflating. She must be in her sixties, Hank thought. Celia went on listening quietly, her eyes small and hopeless, not answering her caller. Hank looked around at the robins on the silk screens, embarrassed for intruding. Someone, perhaps, had died. Her eyes stayed on him. She didn't interrupt.

Hank upset the table and the empty glass of beer when he jumped from the sofa. He grabbed the phone from her hand and listened, not long enough to make out a sentence but long enough to recognize the voice from the service station. He put his hand over the speaker.

"Is there a back way out?"

Her aging eyes were wet and apologetic. She still didn't dare talk. She nodded at the kitchen. The window there closed on a small air conditioner. Chili peppers hung on each side. He took hold of the sash and pulled. It was fastened to the framework with screws. Hank grabbed the top of the sash and pushed so that he could use his leg muscles. He could hear

75

men at the front door and Celia getting up to open it. The screws gave way grudgingly. The sill was old wood and disintegrated under the pressure. The window shot out of Hank's grip and the air conditioner slid out, separating from its wiring and making one full roll before landing on the fire escape.

Hank moved down the escape in jumps, guessing in the dark where the steps were. He hit the ground in a backyard that was one of twenty diminutive backyards surrounded by a wall of houses. It was after supper and too early to go to bed so there were few backroom lights on. He saw a face in Celia's kitchen window looking blindly straight at him. Then the window was blotted out and he heard steps on the escape.

It was an almost tactile dark. He sensed the condensed air of his breath touching his face. The claws of rose bushes snatched at his arms. He ran in a crouch away from the house and the sounds of more men coming down the stairway. The lawn ended abruptly in sharp palings. His foot found a wooden box which he used as a step, coming down in the next yard harder than he expected. He was on concrete. His eyes had adjusted and he looked around, finding the pole and the backboard he expected, like an arrow shot into the ground. He heard the men whispering behind him, arguing whether to use their lights.

Hank crossed the fence to the back yard of a house that faced out on the opposite side of the block, and went on to the next yard. There was a loud scuffle far behind him where a man searching in the other direction had run into a police dog. The sound of barks and garbage can tops mingled. A fainter noise came after. Hank wouldn't have heard it if the man hadn't been so near, slipping over the fence easily. He was only ten feet away, but the dark obscured him and

76

dulled his edges so the gun only made his hand mis-shapen. He didn't see Hank squatting next to a gar-dener's wheelbarrow. In another second the man had gone over the fence to the next yard.

Celia Manx did know it was him. He hadn't con-vinced her, the voice on the phone had. Not that it mattered anymore from what he remembered of the face through her window.

They would be turning on their flashlights soon. It would draw attention, but they were doing that al-ready in the dark. He couldn't get out. There were no alleys or driveways for the ornamental yards, and people in Washington locked their doors and win-dows. He saw the first beam go on in a distant yard, then two others nearer. He nodded; it was what he would have done. He heard a sigh at his back.

At first he thought it was the searcher who had come so near, but as he squinted he made out a figure at the backdoor looking out at the activity. It seemed to stand there forever, a short figure, probably a boy. Finally it opened the door and stood with arms crossed behind a screen door. A luminescent cloud of vaporized breath hid the face. Hank sank back against the wall. He heard a click of metal, and the screen door opened. The figure leaned out.

The doorway was crowded with the two of them, and then Hank was inside, his hand over a mouth. He closed and locked both doors with the other hand. The figure was so light, Hank was practically carrying it in his grip against his chest. They were in a kitchen. He didn't want to turn on lights, so he fumbled in a drawer in the dark for a knife. He found one and put it in his back pocket. He'd left his overcoat and muf-fler in the other house and he needed to replace them. He dragged the figure with him through a dining room and into a living room. There was light coming down the stairs from the second floor, but there were no sounds. He pushed his captive toward the front of the house, maneuvering around the inky reflection of a glass table. He was sure there was a closet by the front door; he could get the clothes and be gone.

"Stop right there and let her go." The voice was vaguely familiar. So was the harsh nudge of a gun in his ribs.

# CHAPTER EIGHT

"We've got the bastards this time. This is their first mistake."

Al Perafini leaned over the glass coffee table to Hank. "What disturbed me right from the start was the interrogation of Halsam. You remember Otto Halsam?"

"Sure," Hank said. "Otto's the attendant at the club."

"Right. Well, in his uncorrected transcript he said that the officers had to pry the .45 from Jameson's hand."

"What does that mean?" Hansen asked.

"It means that it was in his hand when it went off. It's an hysterical reaction of the muscles at the moment of death that you usually find in suicides. The fingers clamp down and won't release even if the rest of the body goes limp."

"Like rigor mortis?" Daisy Hansen asked.

"A very selective rigor mortis," Perafini said. "Sometimes murderers try to fake a suicide by putting a gun in the hand of a victim, but the gun will still fall out when the body is moved. Jameson held onto the gun like it was glued and that man died instantly. No, he shot himself during the fight, like Newman says."

"They corrected the transcript later," Reinhardt said, "when the Duggs Commission got hold of it. Just like they'd like to correct you, Mr. Newman."

Hank looked at Senator Hansen. "You knew all this when you pulled the gun on me?"

"All I knew then was that you were an intruder in my house and you had hold of my daughter."

"That's why you didn't turn me over to the police."

"Let's say I was more inclined to believe your story than most."

"Don't be so modest, Senator," Reinhardt said. "You were the first one to get us looking for Newman when everybody else said he was dead and buried. When they pulled that vanishing act with Celia Manx after you left her, we knew something was rotten in the District of Columbia."

"And what about you, Reinhardt? You're FBI, how did you get involved with this?" Hank asked. Reinhardt grinned sheepishly.

"Even the Bureau has a generation gap," Hansen said.

"J. Edgar can't live forever," Reinhardt said, "and I plan to be looking good when he goes."

"So that's the reason for all this get-together," Hank said. He glanced around the Hansen living room. It had the atmosphere of a war room, with half a dozen agents and legislators mapping strategy. On the walls were no less than a score of photos of Hansen with Presidents and world leaders. Hank felt the germ of an idea coming.

"I know what you're thinking," Daisy said. She nodded to a picture of herself and her father with Celia Manx. "You're right. I'm the person she was expecting when you turned up instead."

"No, that's not what I was thinking," Hank said. "I was wondering what your father expected to get out of this."

A grim line set on Daisy's lips, but her father sighed.

"Don't underestimate him, Daisy," he said. "That's

80

what the enemy did. Yes, it is possible that exposing this plot or whatever it is could embarrass the President. In fact, it almost certainly will. It could ruin his party's chances in next year's elections."

Hansen ran his hand over his face and then through his white hair. The gesture made him appear more tired and old than Hank had thought of him. "It could also mean that I will be nominated by my party, an idea that used to intoxicate me. Now, for the first time, it frightens. I know the President well—we've been at each other's throats long enough, God knows. If he can be this far out of touch with what his people are doing, a clever man like him, then what makes me think that I could do better?"

"You don't think he's behind it?" Reinhardt asked. "I'd assumed—"

"The Senator and I have already gone over this," Perafini said. "The President had everything going for him. Look at the latest polls. Whoever's running this show is operating as if he were running out of time."

"But it still comes down to the elections in '76, doesn't it?" Hank said. "That's what's on your mind."

Hansen called over one of the men who had been studying a roll of representatives spread out on a dining table. He was a bright, bow-tied guy with almost hippie-length hair. Hansen introduced him with the inappropriate name of Hamilton Dill.

"Dill is with the Franklin Institute in Philadelphia. The Institute developed the first computer for the Defense Department during World War II, and has been closely involved with government research in the area ever since. He came to me with an interesting story around Christmas. You think I'm just interested in elections, but maybe this will change your mind."

Dill sat down. He had the confidence of a boy who had gone to college as a full professor.

"I was revising an old paper of mine on the influ-

81

ence of computers on the electoral process," he said. "I wanted to prove my point that systems analysis could bring political campaigns out of the Dark Ages. It just so happened that I got interested in the use of computers to gather votes and project winners of elections and that I happened to pick your fight, the Newman-Porter campaign."

"I remember it," Hank said.

"Then you remember that Porter was picked to win by all the experts. There was what was reported to be a 'difficulty' in the Des Moines computers, actually an IBM 606, though that means nothing to you, and when the results came out, you won in an upset. The experts started drawing graphs about the farm vote, labor, all that. What I did was analyze the returns ward by ward and machine by machine. A kid could have done it. It was so blatant."

"What do you mean?"

"Every tenth vote. You got every tenth vote on every machine according to the Des Moines returns. The odds against that are over a billion to one. That's how you became Representative Newman. Someone punched you in, the way someone would punch an order for hot soup. One martyr coming up."

"You knew this in December?" Hank asked Hansen. "Why didn't you say something then, before I was sworn in? Porter was your friend."

"There have been worse election frauds," Hansen said. "More than one President of the United States has won in spite of votes, Rutherford Hayes being the most outrageous example. Anyway, I felt that you were unaware of the fraud and in times like these it doesn't help to destroy what confidence the public has left in the democratic process. I got Ephram a good position afterward and we just decided to keep an eye on you. Though I'll admit the assassination was a surprise."

"And you knew this, too?" Hank asked Daisy Hansen.

She nodded. Hank sagged in his chair, the wind out of him. He'd never thought of himself as a hero, but he'd never thought of himself as so complete a pawn either. He'd just gone from Duggs to Hansen, that was all. The room, quiet except for the whisper of men adding on sheets of Congressional bond, was a new trap. Twenty-four hours had passed since he had first entered the Hansen house on the run, twenty-four hours for Hansen to assemble his circle, and he knew he wasn't going any further. Georgetown was studded with unmarked patrol cars, and a police boat cruised the Potomac every five minutes. He'd been ordered to stay away from the windows. The Mustang stood where he had left it, just another trap. The police were bound to have traced and bugged it.

"Senator," Dill said, "we're going over the lists again, but we don't see any way to break the twelve vote gap the computer gave us yesterday."

"You don't seem very interested," Daisy told Hank.

"Why should I be?"

"It's the Newman Bill they're talking about."

Hank shrugged. The Newman Bill? Something named after a phony Congressman who became a fake martyr. All he cared about was nailing Duggs.

"We'll just have to fight it in the Senate, that's all," Hansen said. "We still have the edge there."

"Just by five or six, sir, and the President hasn't really come down for it yet."

"That's the difference between you and my father," Daisy said. "He's able to see beyond himself."

"I don't see what the Newman Bill and I have to do with each other," Hank said. "So far as I'm concerned, all that is unreal."

Perafini was on a phone at the other end of the room. When he hung up, sweat had sprouted like a mustache over his upper lip. "Celia is dead. Found in a Baltimore hotel with an overdose of sleeping pills and Scotch."

"That makes two deaths. How real do you want it?" Daisy asked Hank. He was watching Perafini stick his hands in his pockets to keep them from shaking. "Al was the first one Celia called last night to check your story. He blames himself for not coming clean with her."

"What about the second one, George something from the FBI?"

"If you mean George Penty, he was just reassigned to Miami."

"How did the word get out that I was there?"

"Her phone must have been tapped," Reinhardt said from the dining table. "I'm not surprised."

"How do you know the phones here aren't tapped?"

"We check them once an hour. That's the best we can do."

Hansen received a briefcase from one of his aides. He leafed through it rapidly. "I can see that we're reluctant allies, Representative Newman. You find it hard to believe that the issue is greater than your own personal safety, or perhaps you don't care. You think it's merely politics. Time is something we have very little of, but I'm afraid we're going to have to take some of it on a crash re-education program and show you what we think is behind the Newman Bill, behind Mitchell Duggs and certainly behind you."

He handed Hank some pages torn from the Congressional Record of Monday, February 3. Hank recognized it.

"That was a speech I made for the National Data Center Bill."

"If I may quote," Hansen said. "'Are we supposed to wait for another assassin to strike before we finally

84

create an effective defense against this terrorism?" Who wrote that line?"

"Arthur Jameson." He didn't have to think hard. Jameson had done everything for him.

"And who was assassinated and who is the Bill named after now?"

"Me. Granted. I've been through that in my own mind. The problem is that I was for the bill. I still am, as a matter of fact. You have the Record right there. I was one of the main spokesman for the center. The job was handed to me when I got on the Internal Security Committee. So why should I be killed instead of an opponent? It was no life or death issue."

"To someone desperate it was. To you and Jameson and Celia it was."

"The bill had a good chance of passing."

"Now it's almost bound to pass."

"Do you know how much I care?" Hank said slowly.

Daisy Hansen stood up. "Give up, Dad. Here you are arguing with this bandaged ape when who knows what's going on outside. He's not even a Congressman and you, you should have been President ten years ago. You don't need him."

"What do you suggest, Miss Hansen? Throwing me to the wolves? Frankly, I'd be just as happy on my own, but I'm interested in your ethics. A lover of all mankind and goodness but ditch anyone who doesn't think you're Joan of Arc."

"I can see why your wife was so happy to see the last of you," Daisy answered.

"This isn't getting us anywhere, you two," Hansen said. His daughter lowered her eyes to the table. Hank felt the blood pulsing under the gauze on his face. "The fact is that we're all in the same boat and, if you'll permit me to explain, Representative Newman, I'll tell you why. Hamilton, Al, will you join us

85

in my study? I don't want any more tantrums upsetting the work here."

Dill and Perafini trooped out of the living room with expressions of distaste that varied with their professions. Hank preferred the cop's; at least it was human.

"I'd apologize for Daisy's outburst," Hansen told Hank, "but I'm starting to believe you have more than a talent for survival."

"What's that?"

"A death wish. You must have fought like hell to stay alive, but I don't know whether you really give a damn if you make it."

# CHAPTER NINE

"The Secret Service has a bank of 64,000 names. Not just assassins but political activists, 'malcontents,' anyone who might 'embarrass' the President or any other government official. I mean even write something embarrassing in a letter or a newspaper. That's been the official guideline since '68. Their Honeywell pulls out suspects by name, alias, locale, method of operation, affiliation and appearance, and if you think you sound innocent wait until you read a printout on yourself. The data banks get their information from the White House, the Bureau, Army Intelligence, the CIA, the police and its own individual informers. The Honeywell has taps to other SS centers across the country and the SS has the authorization to detain anyone without making a charge," Perafini said.

"I don't see what's wrong with that."

"The Justice Department Civil Disturbance group computer produces a weekly printout of national tension points and 'people of interest.' People of interest means anyone involved in racial controversy and or crime, although the proportion is two to one in favor of controversy. Unless you're Italian," Perafini added with a wicked smile.

"The Department of Housing and Urban Development has a tape on any American who applies for a an FHA loan. It screens applicants through the Justice and FBI files. It also uses its own investigators who solicit information from an applicant's neighbors," Dill said. "All information, good or adverse, is entered and used in determining whether a loan is given. An applicant is not allowed to see the reports."

"That's just bad screening. I agree there should be stricter controls."

"Like Internal Revenue and the Census data?"

"Like Internal Revenue and the Census."

"Dear boy," Hansen said, "the secrecy of IRS tapes is a joke. It has been since the '60s when the Service started to sell its tapes to the states at $75.00 a reel. Prospective jurors have their tax returns checked by prosecuting attorneys. Of course, the IRS requests the states to warn their employees against unauthorized disclosure. And of course, the Census data receives the same strict guardianship."

"Which means the guardianship of the FBI. The Bureau and Customs share twin computers, computers that can print out 100,000 teletype responses in any twenty-four hour period. The Bureau has led the way in electronic surveillance in all fields, including its National Crime Information Center, started in 1966. Its computer talks to 24 regional police computers and to 21 cities and state capitals. It prints out information in the new method: name and alias, social security number, license number and, for purposes of locating a general area where the person can be found and communicating with it, a telephone area code."

"I have to add in defense of the Bureau," Perafini said when Dill had finished, "that it is not the only branch of the government to use electronic surveillance. The Fargo Company, one of the bigger manufacturers, told a Senate committee it sold devices to the Food and Drug Administration, Customs, the Bureau of Narcotics, the Treasury Department, the Atomic Energy Commission, the General Services Administration and the United States Information Agency. Most of the men who use them are trained at the Treasury

Department's Technical Aids School here in the capital. Total sales for taps and bugs come to around $25 million. The results go into the data banks under each person's social security number."

"You probably don't remember, but when those numbers were first introduced, they were supposed to be for social security accounts and nothing else," Hansen said. "Nobody knew then that computers preferred numbers to names."

"You think that computers are malevolent?" Hank asked Dill.

"No, I'm just realistic about humans. The Defense Department had the first computer built during the war so they could win. One reason our defense position is still superior to Russia's is computers, just as American industry is superior to Russia's. There is a world population of 170,000 computers: 100,000 American, 15,000 Russian. And theirs are generally inferior." He seemed to sniff. "The Italians are nearest to us, I suppose. At any rate, we were talking of the uses humans made of computers."

"The Defense Department is still using them but in new ways," Hansen said. "Up till the '60s their computer banks were aimed at external enemies. Now it has a list of 100,000 domestic targets. It was smaller at the start, of course, and there was an overhaul in 1962 when a serviceman in the operation turned out to be a Soviet agent. But then in 1965 a new intelligence command was opened at Fort Holabird, Maryland, just for anti-war reports which came in from eight command posts across the country, each post with 400 agents. In 1967, Holabird became Continental United States Intelligence or Conus Intel, and it had a national teletype dragnet. New data banks were set up at Fort Hood, Texas, and one at Fort Monroe, Virginia. The one at Monroe was called RITA for Resistance in the Army. Around that time officers at Fort Dix, New

Jersey, ordered servicemen to submit to questioning under sodium amytal. Their answers went on file. Conus Intel's mistake was to take on bigger fish, like filing as subversives Senators and Governors. The generals decided they'd better destroy the data banks at Holabird, Monroe and Hood."

"Then what's your point?"

"The order was to destroy everything but one copy."

"In computers that's the same as destroying everything but the negative of a picture," Dill said. "Of course, the data ended up in Monrovia."

"You're telling me that the Army is nuts. That's not news," Hank said.

"That's not all, by a long shot. I just started with them."

"The Army, the Government," Hansen said. "I wish that were all. In your speech you said computers would modernize bureaucracies. It has the opposite effect. Bureaucracies live on data. The more they can get, the more they want. Suddenly everybody wants his own secret computer bank. The state of Oklahoma began its dossier operation in 1968, then came Puerto Rico."

"What did the Justice Department say about all this?" Hank asked.

"I hate to say it," Perafini winced. "Justice gave Oklahoma a giant of $30,000 and Puerto Rico $40,000. But, hell, they go ahead without the grants. California's supposed to be the state of tomorrow. So, Santa Clara county computerized every one of its residents. An official can pull a tape on your name, age, voting status, property, criminal or medical record. California was the first to supply its high schools with two-way mirrors for the washrooms."

"Now it's standard government procedure to send

lists to school guidance counselors for them to reveal students' confidential conversations," Hansen said.

"It's all standard procedure," Dill said. "Are you sick? You're on record with a medical assistance agency or Medicare. Poor? You're monitored by an antipoverty program. The dirtier the secret the more the law demands you tell it. Have you been in the Army, did you ever get a traffic ticket, ever receive a Federal loan, ever been near a demonstration of any kind? You're on tape."

"On tape and there are safeguards in practically every instance to make sure no one makes use of the information," Hank said. "As long as there are men like the senator in Congress I don't think anyone has to worry about his privacy."

"You know, I used to think that, too," Hansen said. "That was before we had the Postmaster General appear before the committee for a hearing on the Open Mail order."

"What's that?"

"It's Post Office Department Form 2008," Perafini said. "It allows any postal inspector—and there are over a thousand of them—to have your mail seized and read without your knowledge. Part of the form says that for public knowledge, the form doesn't exist."

"Not just the public," Hansen said ruefully. "The Postmaster General refused to talk to us about it even after we confronted him with the fact we knew more than a million Forms 2008 were printed for use in 1970. His defense for not answering was Title 39 of the U.S. Postal Code authorized him 'to issue regulations to implement the acts of Congress.' Well, I've looked into it and there never has been an Act of Congress asking for an Open Mail list."

"You know, it's a carefully held secret," Perafini

said in a nasal voice smoothed with irony, "but wire-tapping is illegal, too."

"I doubt that the average person has to worry about having his phone tapped or his mail opened," Hank said. "You want me to feel sorry for every crook or Weatherman?"

"Fine," Hansen said. "Let's say you're an average guy. No controversy, never even had a parking ticket. You've never been in the service and you've never been sick. Then you start to wonder why there's an investigator asking all your neighbors if you drink too much or if you're a homosexual. What's going on?"

"You're getting a credit rating," Perafini slapped Hank on the back. "That's the way they do it."

"Who does it?"

"The credit computers," Perafini said. "There are four giant computerized credit agencies in the United States covering 90 percent of the population. You go into a store in your hometown. Just by picking up a phone they're in touch with the computer at the agency's regional office. In a second your life comes out like a roll of toilet paper. Salary, car, family profile, court record, military record, purchase record, newspaper clippings and rumors. Now, rumors are last but not least. More people are turned down because of rumors than because of the size of their salary. That's why there are two special companies that fill their computers with nothing but rumors that they can sell to the other credit agencies."

Hansen picked it up. "The first good look we had at them in Congress was in 1969. They'd already smeared many Americans. People who would never know why they didn't get a bank loan. People who will never have a chance to see their dossiers to correct them no matter how wild the information against them is."

"Maybe you wondered why a cop would be against

the data bank," Perafini said. "This is part of the reason. It's a lot more profitable for these private data banks just to use everything. The more dirt they have, the more efficient they look. I have some professional pride about that sort of thing."

"So what if I don't want a charge account?"

"It doesn't matter," Perafini said, "just as long as a credit card company or a store or an employment agency is interested in offering you a card or a job. The agencies don't work for you, remember. It's damn easy work, too, I guess that's why so many guys are willing to be investigators. Just find a neighbor who doesn't like your looks. Find out that you were arrested. It doesn't matter if it was a mistake, as one-third of all arrests are. The data banks only carry arrests. Find out if you bought a TV and held up payment. It doesn't matter that you didn't pay because it came without a tube, all the tape says is NO PAY. And if you're really an unfortunate bastard, the computer will just make an error and say you're a sex fiend. That's tough, because computers just won't believe they make mistakes."

"If I might make a point," Dill said, "computers can't. It's just that there are human factors in the programming of the tapes and physical deterioration of equipment. It's not the computers' fault that 3 percent of their operations are in error."

"If I can break into this argument, I'd like to know what all this about credit cards has to do with the National Data Center," Hank said.

"Just this," Hansen said. "After the stores, the main customers of these special banks are the police. Since their business is a little shady, to stay on good terms the agencies give free access to their tapes to any interested official. It all ends up at Monrovia, every bit of it."

"There isn't room for every bit of it," Hank said.

"You made sure of that yourself with the Hansen Resolution. Two years ago Congress limited the amount of information on citizens to 30,000 tapes maximum just so there wouldn't be a lot of junk on them."

Hansen turned to Dill.

"That was before the laser tapes were developed." the computer expert said. "Today you can put a 4,000-word dossier on every American on just 100 1-inch tapes."

Hank, at last, had nothing to say.

"That's the trouble with politicians," Dill continued. "They don't know what they're talking about. How many can explain the difference between an analog or a digital computer? How many know that the difference between a 1st Generation computer and a 5th Generation computer is the same as the difference between an Australopithecine and Homo Sapiens? Perhaps in parts of Borneo tribes exist that still believe in headhunting and barter. Our world is built on computers. Church investments, political donations, dating agencies, everything."

"If I could remind you of something a politician said," Hansen interrupted. " 'The system of espionage being thus established, the country will swarm with informers, spies and all the odious reptile tribe that breed in the sunshine of despotic power. The hours of the most unsuspected confidence, the intimacies of friendship will afford no security. The companion whom you most trust, the friend in whom you most confide, is tempted to betray your imprudence, to misrepresent your words; to convey them, distorted by calumny, to the secret tribunal where suspicion is the only evidence that is heard.' Representative Edward Livingston said that to the 5th United States Congress in 1798." He caught his breath. "As usual, Representative Newman, you don't seem very impressed."

Hank smiled broader than any of them had expected. "You don't mind if I find out whether my reluctant allies can take some hostile questions, do you? Obviously, I should have known what I was talking about when I inflated the Congressional Record, but maybe you should have tried to talk to me before I took a shower with Arthur Jameson."

It was Hansen's turn to be at a loss for words. "I didn't know you could be persuaded then."

"There was nothing in your record to make us think you could be," Dill protested.

"Well, that's the difference between machines and people. People change. I even bounce." He touched his bandage gingerly.

"You better be nice to machines," Perafini said. "They're going to bring you back to life. If all goes according to plan, Representative Newman, you are about to be the first modern case of resurrection."

# CHAPTER TEN

The tent started going up half an hour after sunset. It was an old Army command tent, forty feet by twenty, and it covered about a dozen graves in all. Agents began digging up the turf under the eyes of the grounds foreman. The Colonel who served as acting executive of Arlington stood by ineffectually as the squares of grass were piled carefully into a wall. The grounds keeper complained that the agents weren't doing a proper job despite their care. The dark soil resisted their shovels with frost.

"Should have had heaters out here all day," he said.

The agents, with boots up to their knees, muttered. The Colonel bit his lips. When he opened the flap to look out, one of the agents told him sharply to shut it.

Perafini arrived at 7 with Hank and two Federal marshalls. Hank was in a suit. His bandage was off and the bruise had gone down somewhat, but the center of his face was still puffy and his eyes had a faintly Mongoloid cast. When Representative Mitchell Duggs arrived with an aide and four District Police, he ignored Hank and went to the far end of the tent where a folding table had been set up. The agents were two feet through the cold earth. Battery lamps lit the inside of the tent like the inside of a star. Being driven on the narrow road to the tent, Hank had been struck by how the markers stood out like a neatly arrayed universe.

Duggs waited for a field telephone to be set up on a

smaller table. Hank watched his face for signs of anxiety. Duggs maintained an air of pure annoyance and nothing else. Hank couldn't help the excitement of victory already alive in his stomach. His hands were moist. The tent was warming with body heat and the exertions of the diggers.

"Is the Director coming?" one of the diggers asked.

The man checking the telephone shrugged. He let Duggs talk on it and then asked him if he wanted to wait in his car. Duggs ignored the question. He looked at the growing mound of soil with physical revulsion.

Everett Hansen entered with Reinhardt and Dill and two more marshalls. He viewed the work in operation with approval and sauntered over to Duggs.

"'Lo, Mitchell."

"Hello, Everett. Well, this is quite a mess you started."

Hansen gave the bright scene a second sweep. His eyes rested on Hank for less than an instant but enough for Hank to catch the older man's exhilaration.

"I don't know how you talked the President into this," Duggs said. "All I know is that afterward you might as well make tracks back to Ioway."

"I thought the President would be curious," Hansen said.

"We could have just had Mrs. Newman—"

"Computers don't lie. Or is that your line?" He patted Duggs on the arm. "May the best Representative Newman win."

Hansen walked back to talk with Dill. Duggs glared at the back of his neck. Perafini relieved the two marshalls with Hank.

"If something goes wrong, Hansen is dead in this town. He used every bit of political capital he had to force the President into this. From now on it's his

97

neck," he told Hank in a low voice. "Yours too, of course."

"What about you?"

"Guarding the pipeline in Alaska, I guess," Perafini admitted.

"Why is Dill along?"

"They're bringing in a mobile relay to Monrovia to get the word. A programmer will come with it to punch in the two sets of data and find out which of you is for real. The Senator wanted Dill along to make sure the punching's done in accordance with the Marquis of Queensbury rules. Once the punching's started, the whole show will practically be over."

"What do you think the odds are?"

Perafini lifted an eyebrow. "This is a hell of a time for you to start having doubts. A hundred to zero, so far as I can see. If they were any worse, I think Representative Duggs would have some friends around to share the gloating. He's alone. That's the best sign I've seen so far. Just keep cool."

The mound of fresh dirt was almost waist-high. A tall, thin man with a white crew cut entered the tent. Hank recognized Dr. John Akers, Surgeon General. Mitchell Duggs and Everett Hansen both welcomed the doctor warmly, but he was plainly upset by the entire project and he seemed to blame them equally. "Harebrained" was the kindest adjective Hank caught. He had instead of a black bag a narrow metal case. He set it down on the long table and opened it. Hank could see that besides the usual apparatus, the case contained an unusual number of knives.

Another man arrived soon afterward. He conferred with Hansen and Duggs and left. A few minutes later Hank heard a motor. The flaps were opened to reveal the back of a small van equipped with a hydraulic lift. The man reappeared with a friend to open the van door and push forward a squat console. They

98

lowered it with the lift and, with the help of two agents, pushed it over the grass. From the effort needed and the deep ruts left, Hank was made aware of the machine's weight. He knew what it was because there had been five of them in the House chamber.

A thick coil was attached to the back of the console and run up to the generator still in the truck. Dill and his opposite from Duggs watched the programmer check out the circuits.

"How long?" Hank asked when Dill wandered by.

"Fifteen, twenty minutes. The computer's ready as soon as you turn the juice on. It's just the tubes for the panel that have to warm up."

The questions and answers could have been done over a Bureau radio, Hank knew. It just proved Hansen wasn't taking chances of any kind.

An agent approached Hank with a camera and took light readings of his face.

"Might as well get this over with now, sir," he said. "Looks like you need a new baseball glove."

"Maybe I'll just take out more insurance."

The agent laughed and stepped back. He snapped pictures of Hank's face from the front and both sides. It took Hank a second to realize they were the necessary angles of mug shots.

An old man with a deeply seamed face pushed his way through the flaps. He wore a hat with a down-turned brim that was out of style by forty years, but he walked briskly to the Surgeon General. The Bureau's Director wasn't coming but the Second in Command had. He said nothing but surveyed the tent with eyes hidden in pits, one hand over the other. The diggers redoubled the efforts. Everyone acted as if Hank weren't there until a young, prematurely bald man showed up. He stared at Hank through thick glasses for a full minute before joining the rest at the table. From their conversation, Hank gathered the newcomer was the White House liaison. He used the phone and everybody fell silent while he talked.

An agent led Hank to a chair in a corner of the tent and told him to strip to the waist. A seam of cold air slipped through the canvas and Hank felt goose bumps rising as he took his jacket and shirt off. Dr. Akers, pulled up a chair next to him.

"Okay, Mr. X, hold out your arm."

Hand expected a needle. The doctor simply brought out a sphygmomanometer and a stethoscope. He wrapped the first around Hank's forearm and applied the second to his chest.

"Why not a lie detector instead of blood pressure?" Hank asked.

"Polygraph? Too simple to fake, just flex your feet and it says what you want it to. Drugs? Hypnosis takes care of that, and if you're some sort of super-spy, you have that. I'll take the tried and true, thank you. Don't blink, please." He shined a light into Hank's pupils. He went on garrulously as he gave Hank a thorough physical.

"You're a G.P.," Hank guessed.

"That's right. Probably why they made me Surgeon General, to show off an antique. When I die they'll hang me from the ceiling at the Smithsonian like one of those biplanes. In ten years there won't be any doctors, just midwives and computers. Drop your pants please."

Hank had just finished dressing when a shovel hit the casket. The tempo of the diggers increased. The grounds keeper stood by with a pair of ropes. Hank's face became darker with the blood rushing through it. The only one not affected by the sound of the shovels around the edges of the casket was Dill. He sat at the display panel, feeding it questions. Both questions and answers showed up on the panel in a stilted language of algebra-English. The one exception was the

100

last exchange. Dill ordered, COMPLÉTE: I TEACH YOU THE SUPERMAN. The answer appeared as the question faded from the screen. MAN IS SOMETHING TO BE SURPASSED.

"I think we've got it," one of the agents in the grave said. All that could be seen of the diggers was their heads and shoulders. The grounds keeper passed down the first rope, then the second. The marshalls helped once the ropes were in place, hoisting the coffin up out of the hole. When it was level with the ground, they walked it forward and set it down. The Bureau Assistant Director made a barely audible noise and an agent jumped out to open the lid. It wouldn't budge. He searched for a lock without success and tried again. It still wouldn't open.

"It's sealed," the agent said.

"No," the grounds keeper said. "You just don't know what you're doing. Think you can just come in and run the show without the least idea of necrohygienics. Right, Colonel?"

The cemetery administrator, shunted aside till now, nodded fiercely. It was hard for Hank not to smile at the struggle of jurisdictions on a cold night in Arlington. The people involved were not amused.

"This is one of the newest caskets," the grounds keeper said. "Don't need any screws or locks. You've got a vacuum in there. Lock and preservative in one. *Regard.*" He stepped to the foot of the long, silvery coffin and located a small valve hidden in scrollwork. He turned it and a sharp hiss sucked at the air. The lid stirred with a faint pop. "It's all yours."

Hank held his breath and saw Duggs and Hansen doing the same. Two agents lifted the casket lid slowly and swung it back. Hank made out a pair of shoes. One agent reached in and grabbed the body under the knees, the other one took the shoulders. Arthur Jameson came out, sagging at the middle. His face was serene even as his arms swayed.

"Don't let his hands drag!" the Colonel snapped.

They lifted him higher. It was difficult because the dead weight slumped in a new direction every time they improved their hold on it. Finally the grounds keeper helped them deposit their burden on the table. From the expression on his face, it was plain he could get a job at a private cemetery without any trouble.

Dr. Akers unbuttoned the corpse's jacket and shirt. Hank noticed that the suit on Jameson was his own. All the clothes were except for the shoes. Jameson was just a little shorter and broader. Hank hadn't thought about it in the shower.

Dr. Akers had performed autopsies before. After measuring the body with a green tape, he immediately opened up the chest cavity. Long needles held the folds of skin and subcutaneous fat back as he probed inside with a variety of instruments. He'd removed his jacket, but he didn't bother to roll his shirt cuffs.

"What are you doing that for?" Duggs asked irritably.

"Just making sure this man died the way he's supposed to. If he didn't, that would raise some questions, wouldn't it?" Jameson didn't seem to have decomposed, but there was a bland lifelessness to his body, as the scalpels sliced through it, that made him seem not so much dead as not there. There was no blood because it had been drained, and the vegetable coloring of the formaldehyde that had replaced it had faded.

There were none of the alterations to Jameson's face that Hank had suspected, nothing in the way of plastic surgery for Akers to discover. The answer was simple. The only people in the tent who knew Jameson were Duggs and himself. Records on the press secretary had been sequestered by Duggs' commission. Hank corrected himself. There was someone else in the tent who knew and had all the records. Monrovia. Akers closed up the chest and began inspecting the rest of the body.

"Eleven o'clock, sir," one of the agents said. Akers wouldn't be hurried. He took Jameson's shoes off and inspected the toes. Hank saw why they hadn't forced his shoes on Jameson. The poor fit would have left its marks. He swallowed and thought everyone could hear his dry throat. The heels of the shoes had a pattern of studs in them that Hank had never seen before. It would have been pointless to mention, though. The issue was not going to be decided by whether the dead man's shoes were his or not.

Akers let an agent replace socks, shoes, and pants. He busied himself examining Jameson's teeth, noting on a pad which had fillings and of what kind. He looked into the ears, turning the head first one way and then the other. Finally he looked at the eyes, sliding their lids back with his thumbs.

Hank started. The dead man's eyes were dull, as if they were looking out instead of in, and they were green. Jameson's eyes were brown.

"That's the wrong body," Hank said. Everybody turned to him. "My press secretary had brown eyes."

Akers relaxed.

"I've no doubt. After a while following death, all Caucasian eyes become greenish."

The doctor closed the lids carefully with his thumbs. Then he wiped his hand on a large, old-fashioned kerchief.

"Are you done?" Duggs asked.

Akers put his jacket on before he said, "Yes. I've made notes of the significant differences between the two men. There's little point, I assume, in running over those physical characteristics that are shared. Both men are, or were as the case may be, in very

103

good physical condition." He pulled a cheroot out of his jacket. "Must have been quite a fight." He handed his notes to an agent, who took them to the programmer already sitting at the computer console.

Dill and Duggs' man stood over the programmer's shoulder as he punched in the first match-up of data. "X=73IN+BP130/95STOP=72IN+BPNA"

"Z=73IN" the display answered.

Duggs touched his lips nervously. Perafini winked at Hank. More symbols appeared on the screen. Hank found his breathing evening out. X, Y and Z. X was agreeing more with Z than Y and he knew by now that Jameson was Y. Akers remarked that the variance was not conclusive, that a man always changed somewhat between examinations and nothing changed a man more than death. The way he said it did not encourage Duggs.

"X = CARIESUR3M + LL1MSTOPY = CARIE SUR2M + LL1M"

"Z=CARIESLL1M"

Akers raised his eyebrows. Hansen looked at Hank.

"I had a filling put in a month ago," Hank said.

"The dead man could say the same thing," Duggs said.

More symbols splashed over the screen. The only sound was the programmer's fingers on the keyboard and the whirr of the generator outside the tent.

"X=BLTYP'O'STOPY=BLTYPENA"

"Z=BLTYPE'O'"

"X=FPR-W,L,L,W,A; FPL-W,L,C,L,L STOPY= FPR-W,C,C,W,L;FPL-L,C,A,L,L"

"This could be it," Perafini whispered to Hank. "Fingerprints. The letters stand for whorls, loops, arches and composites."

The display took longer to answer. When it did it said "Z=NA"

"Not available?" Hansen said. "What's going on here?"

"EXPLAIN" the programmer punched.

"NASTOPMEDRECCOUNCILBLUFFIOWAVET-ERANSHOSP FIRE STOP MILREC DESTROYED-PACIFISTSSTOP NOCRIMREC"

"Ask for Jameson's record," Hank said.

"Our agreement was that only questions about the identity of Representative Newman would be asked," Duggs said.

"Go ahead," Dill said. He was more shaken than Hank, if possible.

Hansen and Duggs both turned to the Bureau AD. Hank could only see the AD's eyes by their reflected light. The old man opened his mouth. A thin line of teeth showed.

"Go ahead," he said.

"REQUEST REC ARTHUR JAMESON," the programmer punched.

"ARTHURJAMESON ADDRESS19459541130 REP 2105TODAY APPREHENDEDSANFRANCALBY FBI"

Lips closed over the thin teeth and formed a small smile. "That's all we need to know about Jameson," the AD said. "Get on with the rest of it."

More symbols danced over the screen. In general, his agreed more with Z than the dead man. He was scared, though. Z was no longer himself in Hank's mind. It was someone else he didn't know and the agreement was only by chance. The fear was irrational but he couldn't shake it. Z was a fickle electronic ghost waiting to play its joke.

It came before Hank had prepared himself.

"X=MELPIGDAM F/BSTOPY=MELPIGDAM F"

"Z=MELPIG DAM F B"

"Pigmentation damage of that sort can correct itself

over the long run," Akers said. "Otherwise, we'd all go around with permanent tans."

Hansen seemed to think it was significant and so did Perafini. They were saying so when the next array of symbols appeared.

"Z=NIRISPIGDAM"

It was an answer where there had been no question.

"Iris?" Hansen asked. "You just said the eyes had changed color."

"On the dead man," Dill said. "Z is Newman. Newman's eyes might have changed color but didn't. For some reason."

"Spit it out," Akers told the man at the console.

"UNKNOWN QUANTITY=A STOPA+Z=POSIRISPIGDAM STOPDEF A"

"SURGDETRET+X=POSIRISPIGDAM"

"I missed it. It must have been a good job," Akers said testily. He glanced at Hank. "It's harder when they're dead but that's no excuse."

He went back to the body on the table. Hank turned to Perafini.

"Operation for a detached retina," the Justice man said unemotionally. "Machine says you had it."

"Clouded, dehydrated, but the scars are there," Akers said. He closed the lids. The unexpectedly green eyes seemed to wink. Dill had the console repeat, "Z=NIRIS PIG DAM" Hansen looked back and forth. "I don't get it, this is the first time the corpse came close," he said. Dill stared at the screen with disbelief.

"Close enough," Akers said, "I'll tell you, your man fooled me. He really did." He snapped his case shut. "You might as well put Representative Newman back in your grave."

"Wait. That's it?"

PIG DAM still glowed on the screen.

"Representative Newman had an operation to re-attach a retina, an operation that very rarely disturbs the pigmentation of the iris. The dead man had such an operation on his left eye. Your man didn't, it's as simple as that. Did you?" Akers asked Hank.

"No."

"Looks like it's all over," Duggs said. Rivulets of sweat ran down the wings of his nose.

"There's no point in going on, Senator," Akers said gently. "You were fooled, too. You can't deny the facts." He turned back to Hank, "It wasn't such a stupid mistake. I guess we should be thankful."

Perafini tapped the programmer's back. The screen faded. Two agents stationed themselves by Hank's side. They didn't put handcuffs on him, but he had no doubt about his status. The AD was on the phone. He handed it to the Surgeon General.

"Awful mess, yes, sir," he said. "I don't know how." The cable was pulled out of the console's back. Duggs was next on the phone. Hansen stood in front of Hank.

"Now I see," he said. "You were in with Duggs the whole time. The chase with the police, killing Celia, it was all a setup." He would have hit Hank, but it would have made him appear even more ridiculous.

"I never had an operation," Hank said, shaking his head.

"I know," Hansen said.

"It lied. The computer lied."

Hank thought the Senator was too angry to say anything else. Hank was wrong. "Computers can't lie," Hansen whispered. "But don't you wish they could?"

Duggs hung up. He composed his face from one of joy to sorrow. "The President didn't have time to talk to you, Everett. I gave him your apologies."

"Thank you, Mitchell. That was kind," Hansen said.

He wasn't as upset when he didn't have to look at Hank.

"I'll have the Director talk to the Attorney General in the morning," the AD told Perafini.

"Very good," Perafini said. It was nice to know in advance when your career came to an end.

The console was rolled onto the lift at the same time the coffin was lowered into the grave. "About time," the groundskeeper said. The phone was taken out of the tent with the AD. Akers left. Perafini and Dill left with Senator Hansen. None of them cast a backward glance at Hank. He heard the truck roll down the road and then the sounds of the cars. Finally, the agents took him by the arms and led him outside.

It was cold. He'd forgotten. The cemetery reflected the starry sky. There were just a few cars left on the road. The three of them started down to it.

"Wait a second, boys." Mitchell Duggs moved down from the tent and joined them. "I'd like to talk to the prisoner alone for a second."

"We're not supposed to let him out of our sight, sir."

Duggs looked around. "It's a bright night. You'll see if he tries anything."

After a moment's hesitation, the agents moved about twenty feet away on each side with their jackets open.

Hank rubbed his arms.

"Cigaret?" Duggs said.

"Thanks."

Duggs lit two and gave Hank one.

"Not like that night on the *Onthaloosa*, is it? Boy, you sure gave us enough trouble, Hank. Aren't you relieved it's over? Lord knows I am."

"What happens now to Senator Hansen?"

"I wouldn't worry about him if I were you. He's just

dead politically. You've been dead officially twice in one week. That's some sort of record."

"Why? Why did you fix the votes? Jameson? Just for that bill?"

"The Newman Bill, Hank. Let's not be modest. You should see this place in the spring. Crocuses all over."

"Come on, Mitchell, what does it matter now? Tell me what it's all about."

Duggs watched the taillights swing through the gate far away. "It's very important. That's all I can tell you. I wouldn't have put you through this if it weren't, believe me."

"You mean you wouldn't have me killed now if it weren't."

Duggs dropped his cigaret in the grass and stubbed it out with his shoe. "Nobody's having you killed, Hank. This time you're dead for good. Go where you want, say what you want, you can't touch us. Tonight finished any possibility of that. Stand on the Capitol steps if you care to. Nobody's going to want to be another Everett Hansen. This time you're not only dead but buried."

"What makes you so sure?"

"Watch and find out," Duggs said. He walked back to the tent before Hank could ask him any more questions.

The agents put Hank in a car and drove out of the cemetery. The roads were nearly deserted, and he anticipated another ride in the country. Instead, they joined the lane going into the city. He saw the first floodlit government building as they crossed the Potomac into the city proper. More government offices swam by like white whales in a dark sea. The agents were in no hurry. They stopped at red lights like everyone else. Kids came out of an all-night theater, their laughs carrying. The agents talked about baseball, paying no attention to Hank. The Washington

Monument was straight ahead, growing and receding at the same time as they approached. A weird coziness had settled in the car.

The traffic was congested even at the late hour around DuPont Circle. Stalled drivers watched the colored fountain in the center change from orange to red to blue. The agents' car had just started moving again when Hank dove through the door. He was gone when the driver's hand reached his gun and stopped.

Hank ran at a crouch through the slow-moving cars and onto the island in the center of the circle. He crept around the kaleidoscope fountain, keeping his eye on the agents' car through the cascade.

Suddenly the fountains died and he was looking directly at the driver's face. The agent laughed. The traffic began moving again and the car went with it.

Hank stood up as the water shot into the air. Some drops fell on him before he stepped back. Like a photograph left too long in a developing pan, he disappeared into the darkness.

# CHAPTER ELEVEN

On a vast construction site on 9th Street was the new Justice Department Building. The charred, uninhabited temple of concrete and steel would have been the fifth largest government edifice in terms of floor space, file cabinets, air vents, telephone wires, garage facilities and recirculated plumbing if it had opened as scheduled in 1972. The bombs of 1972, 1973, and 1974 had changed the schedule and the work still went on in a building that had become a fossil. And across 9th Street still existed the Skid Row that the city planners had meant to crush with the almighty boot of the colossal building.

There was nothing uninhabited about the seamy side of the street. The transient hotels had to turn away men from chicken wire bins, and the bars offered free sausage with California Port. There was industry, too, a heady trade in blood donors, dishwashers and, for the very ambitious, trucks that took daylaborers to farms in three states. In the first week after being let go — he didn't kid himself about escaping — Hank tried them all. He tried hitching to Iowa the week after that. He was calling his old law partner collect from Chicago, when he got someone else instead. It was the voice from the filling station phone. As one friend to another, it said, there was a warrant for his arrest as soon he stepped over the Iowa border. It even gave him the name he'd be arrested under and the crime. Theft of credit cards. It offered to read the warrant to him. Hank asked the voice if it wasn't afraid of using up its three minutes. It didn't answer. It wasn't as if the voice couldn't think of anything to say, Hank felt, as much as the space of silence was for a laugh. Only there was no laugh, just the space for it. Hank didn't have to worry about the operator, the voice went on. By the way, it added, his widow was already engaged. To his law partner.

Hank went to Union Station and bought a Des Moines paper. He turned to the social page. The voice had been right. On the front page he found some other news. Senator Hansen had temporarily returned home to recuperate from a sudden illness. No details were divulged, but it was not predicted when he would go back to his duties in Washington. On the station board the times were posted for trains heading to Los Angeles, Ontario, Albuquerque, New York and Washington. Four choices for the future and one to the past. That was how Hank ended up back on 9th Street. It occured to him that a coward always preferred his future to facing his past, even if everyone was willing to help him believe it didn't exist.

He was smarter the second time. He avoided the employment agencies that divided men into dishwashers and squat laborers. Between the bars and the local police station he discovered a walk-up office full of bail bondsmen. The door to the office said, *"Vatjes a Puerto Rico y Venezuela*—Income Tax Service—Driving School—Bail Posted."

"You're not the first broken-down lawyer in the world," E. O. Bernhardt said. He was the stereotype of the shyster lawyer: fat, serge-suited and talking through a cigar. With one exception. He was black. "Have you got a name?"

"William Poster."

Bernhardt missed his nose once but not twice. With his finger probing one nostril he sounded like a broken organ. "Had a white guy until a week ago. Liver gave out. You drink?"

112

Hank shook his head. Now that the question was asked, he wondered why he hadn't started.

"Doesn't matter," Bernhardt said. He inspected his finger. Hank looked around at the office. It was decorated with travel posters of San Juan and the laws and penalties on jumping bail. "We'll find out soon enough. You can have that desk." He pointed out a desk even more buried under paper than the others. It was close to the door and there was a baseball bat beside the chair. Hank grasped that his size had as much to do with the job as whatever legal training he had.

"How much is the pay?"

Bernhardt was so dramatically shocked, Hank caught the aptness of the name. "Money! We'll wait a week and find out why you're on 9th Street. I mean, if you were Perry Mason, you wouldn't be here. You follow me?"

The work was simple, merely keeping tabs on how much money was available to Bernhardt's runners down at the District Court. They called in and he told them how high they could go and whether the bail demanded by a judge was so high for a particular crime that he was asking for a payoff. A disgruntled client came through the door once with a gun in his hand. Hank knocked it out with the bat and Bernhardt, moving with amazing speed for a man built like a bathtub, cleaned the client up in a matter of seconds. The gun was empty, but that was the day Bernhardt started paying Hank.

Hank developed an odd affection and admiration for the bondsman. Bernhardt was a crook—the interest on the money he put up was blatant extortion—but the system he was operating in was more crooked. Bernhardt would lean out the window and look at the unfinished Justice Building down the street. "Isn't that beautiful? Wanted to have all those bright little lawyers and cute little secretaries running in and out of doors. Maybe a little park where we are right now. Box hedges. Nice and clean and bright, you know what I mean. Like a nice, healthy million-ton white boy with a college degree. And look at it. It's falling down in its hole. Got to have guards to keep the winos out. Can't do anything about the rats, you know. Yes sir, it ends right there. They can't go any farther. Could have used that money to get ten thousand men out of jail, but that's what they wanted and that's what they got."

Bernhardt became interested in Hank. "You're like that building, you know that?"

"I handle the phone and the bat. I don't have to be your straight man."

"White boy all messed up. Only you've got a bit of the unknown quantity in you, some mystery. What did you do? You're no bum. Not a thief, you would've stolen something by now if you were. No crumpled look like an alimony skipper."

"That worries you?"

"Damn right it does. Just about all that leaves is murder. But if that was it, the cops would have you by now. See, a man like you comes to this part of town only when he's on the run. But you're not running, I can see that. Why is that, Mr. Poster?"

"Because they know where I am."

"As if that answers a goddamn thing." Bernhardt threw his hands up.

A few days later Bernhardt approached and threw his hands up again. "Talk about being straight men. 'Bill Poster will be prosecuted.' Goddamn."

Hank got a room in one of the better transient hotels. Most of them had 8-by-4 metal cages with a cot and a locker. His had real rooms with beds and bureaus and a toilet that worked at the end of the hall. He used Bernhardt as his banker. It was safer, he

114

decided, and the interest was better. In the evenings he would pass up the attractions of the 8mm. blue movies shown in the cellars and the gamut of bars and ride a bus to whatever branch of the public library was open. He did not apply for a library card to take a book out. Six weeks after the night in the cemetery he was starting to understand things and he thought he should act.

The Georgetown bus stopped at the bridge. He walked the rest of the way, following the river. It was after work and almost dusk when he came to the spot where he had left the Mustang long ago. The Hansen house looked deserted. He wasn't surprised because the papers said the Senator was still recuperating in Iowa. There was a For Sale sign on the front lawn. Hansen apparently intended to be sick for sometime more.

There were no cars parked near the house, no men reading Jeane Dixon. He crossed the street and walked up to the front door. He tried the doorbell. It was disconnected. The door was unlocked, though, giving way as he brushed against it. The musty smell of an unused house seeped out as he stepped in. Maybe the realtor selling it had left it unlocked for a customer, Hank thought. He was lucky, but he didn't have much time. He climbed the stairs to the second floor. He had stayed in the bedroom on the left. Passing down the hall, he noticed the pattern of squares and circles left on the walls by missing pictures. He thought of Jameson's dead eyes.

"You! What are you doing here?"

Daisy Hansen stepped out of a bedroom dressed in a halter and shorts.

"Hello."

"I said, what are you doing here?" She was squeezing a pair of scissors in her hands hard enough for the knuckles to turn white. The improbable thought crossed Hank's mind that she was capable of attacking him.

"I forgot something."

"You didn't forget anything. You ruined my father, humiliated him so that he can't even stay in this town, ruined the careers of half a dozen other people and got your bill through. Don't tell me you forgot anything," she said bitterly.

"I'm sorry about your father."

"Don't say it," Daisy said. "Don't or I'll kill you. I will and I'll be proud of it."

"I don't doubt you."

"Get out."

"I'll do that. I just want to get something I left here."

"You had a month to do that. You don't have to do it now. Duggs can wait."

"I can't. There's something I have to look for. I apologize. I didn't know you were here, but now I have to get it. I'm going into the bedroom and if you want to kill me go right ahead."

He tried to step around her. She stabbed him in the shoulder but he went by into the room. The scissors dropped on the floor, the tips daubed red, and she picked them up. He opened a bureau drawer. It was empty.

"You're crazy."

"Maybe. I've considered it." He opened another empty drawer. "Your father's a great man but he's not here, Daisy. I'm the only one left, and someone has to carry on the good fight."

His broad back was a good target but he ignored her, busy with the drawers. It was like a dream she'd had a hundred times, only reality was more frightening, more confusing.

"What do you mean, carry on the fight? You still claim you're Howard Newman?"

"Yes, but you can call me Hank." He finished with the bureau and pulled a suitcase from under the bed. She crept up behind him with the scissors. "Be careful. Getting it between the ribs can be tricky."

She stepped back as he put the suitcase in the center of the room. He opened it up and sorted through the contents, mostly toilet articles. He looked up at her and grinned. "Remember, you asked me once if things didn't seem too easy for me?"

"When was that?"

"When I talked to you and Celia Manx at the club. Well, things aren't easy now. You've got enough junk in here to stock a dump."

"You still think you're Newman."

"So do you." He finished with the suitcase and went to a cardboard box in the corner.

Daisy was more uncertain than she cared to admit. The house had been empty for a month, plenty of time for Duggs and his stooge to ransack it. Duggs certainly would have known that she had returned to Georgetown when he sent the stooge over. Unless there was some reason for carrying on the charade, and there wasn't because as a political force her father was dead. There was no sense to it.

"Why do you say that?" she asked.

The box was full of towels and sheets. "Because I can feel how you feel. You took a violent dislike to me when we met at the club. I don't know why, unless I'm particularly unlovable. But it's there, it's there right now."

"You were an arrogant, cocky bastard the first time I met you and you still are."

"See what I mean?" He laid the sheets out on the bed.

"You can't be Representative Newman. They proved you weren't," Daisy protested. This wasn't at all the way she'd dreamed their confrontation.

117

"Who did?" Hank looked up.

"The computer."

"Well, who are you going to believe?"

"You or the computer?" Daisy asked.

"No. *You* or the computer."

The box was empty and he started putting the linen back in it. "What in the world are you looking for?" Daisy asked in frustration.

"A little white card. It was in my jacket when I came here. It seemed unimportant and I never got to mention it to your father. Not that it would have made a difference."

"You had some things I didn't pack. I threw them in the trash."

"Where?"

Daisy thought it over and pointed at the hall. Hank crossed into the opposite bedroom and found plastic bags stuffed with everything Daisy was not taking to Des Moines. He looked back at her and she shrugged.

"There'll be a lot less mess if you can remember which bag." The desire to have him out of the house won. She kicked a bag near the door. "Thanks."

The card was halfway down in the bag. It looked folded, bent and mutilated but it was the same one, blank and anonymous. He put it in his pocket.

"Are you going to leave now?"

Hank went down the stairs without making any good-byes. She wasn't in the mood for words, and he didn't blame her.

"You know, if you ever do prove you are Representative Newman you've got a surprise coming," she said from the top of the stairs. Her hands were on her hips and she shot the words at him like bullets. "Nobody's going to care."

He followed the dark braid of the Potomac back to the city.

# CHAPTER TWELVE

He knew the girl was only trying to be cruel, but the words had their effect. The odds against his proving anything were so astronomical as to be ridiculous. And if he did, who cared?

The Newman Bill had passed the Senate 66-26. When the President returned from his European tour in another week, he would sign it into law. He wanted it. The American Manufacturers Association had lobbied for it as strongly as the Defense Department. *Time* said that no one could deny computerization had kept American business strong and maybe it could do the same for government. The so-called Church League, which had kept computer files on "radicals" for years, said the nation's very morality depended on it. On the other hand, the Communist Party of the United States approved the data center. House and Senate liberals told chicken dinners of the Americans for Democratic Action that computers were, in the words of Representative Fien, "safeguards of civil rights, sentinels of sanity." The NAACP said "computerization is integration." The only opponents were a handful of political mavericks who claimed there was something pernicious in turning over decision-making to machines. They didn't understand that in 1975, after the unending years of war and crime and drugs and hearing about the poor and racism and feeling that elections only changed

119

men not policies, the people were willing to do just that.

He sat by the door of Bernhardt's office and told himself that the girl was just vindictive and that he was right and everyone else was wrong. This way leads insanity, he thought, and he was happy when one of the runners called with a problem in geography. A George Jackson had just been hit with a bail set at $25,000 for a compound case of bigamy.

"I agree, the judge went overboard," Hank said. He nodded at Bernhardt as he came in with his bookkeeper. "It's a shakedown, yeah, especially considering that Jackson lives on his veteran's disability allowance. He's pretty unlikely to give that up. Let me think." He held his hand over the phone.

"What's up?" Bernhardt asked.

"This guy is an amputee but he still managed to get himself a wife in Baltimore, a wife in Richmond and one here in the Capital. That must have kept him hopping. Anyway, the judge set a wild bail considering the man's disability, which is his entire income. I don't see what we can do for him."

Bernhardt nudged his book keeper, an alcoholic named Peecen. "You want to see an A No. 1 criminal mind at work, watch this. Missed his calling, he should have been a priest."

"The District wife was first?" Hank asked the runner. "That's the bad part. They're tough here. No divorce for cruelty, drink, impotence, fraud, nonsupport. You have to be caught ravishing the President's secretary at high noon on the Senate steps. The judge can get away with that sort of blackmail. Why in the world did Jackson let on that he had a third wife stashed away? Look, this guy seems to have a habit. Where is he from?"

Bernhardt looked on like a proud teacher. Hank glanced at him and winced.

"Delaware? Okay, ask him if he can remember a wife there. Tell him to cut the crap, is there a wife there or not? . . . Fine, everything is in confidence. . . . I can do without the details. . . . No, it won't increase his sentence if he tells us. . . . Right, to change court. And Delaware's perfect. It's one of the few states where bigamy is grounds for divorce. Plug in the Public Defender to this, get him up to Dover with Jackson's military record and we can have some character witnesses by then. If things work out we can finish a divorce up there when we want and come down on another judge's calendar here. . . . Okay, okay, just tell the Defender what I said." He hung up.

"See what I mean," Bernhardt said, "I ought to charge legal fees." He thought it over. "Maybe Jackson could use some driving lessons."

Gerald Peecen was a thin, pinkish man with a red nose. His cuffs and collars were severely starched. The combination was vaguely that of a candy cane. He was a wizard bookkeeper during the day, when he was sober. After work, he regularly drank himself to a stupor and tried to get Hank to join him. He was shocked when Hank finally agreed.

"Are you sure? Is something wrong?" Peecen asked.

"No," Hank laughed. "I'm just in the mood." It had been two days since he'd seen Daisy Hansen and he'd been unable to concentrate since.

They went out on 9th Street, and wove their way through citizens breathing heavily on a plate glass window. Inside, a projection box was showing a trailer for the movie in the cellar. Signs on the window invited "Serious Mature Clientele Only." The books on the shelves ranged from *The Sin of Mrs. O* to *The Naked and the Dead.*

"Consider the advantages of vices, and booze always comes out ahead," Peecen said. "You can enjoy it in the most dignified surroundings or the shabbiest, with friends or in solitude, in gay moods or depressions It encourages the free flow of ideas, it builds confidence in one's self and trust in one's fellow man, and its consumption provides vital tax revenue for the state. I can think of only one vice that vies with it and that is religion, and religion doesn't taste good."

"I see you're a university man," Hank said.

They came to Peecen's grail, a less shoddy tavern on a side street, and secured two stools at the bar. The bartender asked Peecen whether he still had a job and then served them.

"The eighth sin," Peecen said, "is credit."

"I haven't had a boilermaker in a year," Hank said as he chased his whiskey with beer.

"Please," his companion grimaced. "The very idea chills me." He was already into his second.

They drank and talked for an hour, Peecen growing increasingly eloquent. Hank enjoyed him. The bookkeeper was obviously intelligent, and he wondered what he had been before ending up as Bernhardt's assistant. Other habitues of the bar called him "professor" and once the bartender told him a school was trying to locate him and left a phone number to call. Peecen tore the slip up.

"You might say that I'm on sabbatical," he told Hank. "That is to say, I was canned at the last place and I'm taking advantage of my disadvantage as long as I can. Then I'll have to go back to some, groan, job where I have to wear a tie."

"What do you teach, English, mathematics?"

"When I instruct, both in a fashion. I am a programme instructor."

"He's a genius," the bartender put in. "In about a month, when they figure he's ready to dry out, the guys from IBM will be here again."

Hank put his glass down, untouched. "That's interesting," he said casually.

"It's fascinating," Peecen said. "It's the Brave New World and the Great American Novel wrapped up in one magnetic tape. Don't tell me."

"Sure." Hank searched in his jacket. It was still there, the punched card he'd taken from Jameson's body, that he'd taken again from Senator Hansen's house. "Maybe you could help me. I found this computer card the other day. I was wondering what it said."

"Simple enough." The flourish of Peecen's red nose as he took the card indicated that he was being asked to add one and one.

"There aren't any indications about what any of the holes mean."

"Not to you," Peecen said. "However, it's quite plain. There are 80 vertical rows of 9 spaces each. The first 30 rows are for numerals. The next 26 are for letters of the alphabet. All the rest are for whatever special code the user of the card wants. See? So, we look at the numerals first. There are 12 punches. The numbers are 1, 5, 6, 3, 0, 2, 1, 0, 7, 2, 0, 2. Got that?"

Hank nodded. The first nine numbers were his social security number. His mind went on to the last three numbers and came up with a device of the National Crime Information Center: 202 was the Washington area code.

"The words. The alphabet is broken up into 3 groups by the computer, 9, 9 and 8. Look, the first letter here is N. You can tell because above the row there's a punch for the second letter-group. In the row there's a punch five stops down. N is the fifth letter of the second letter-group. N, as in another one," he told the bartender.

"And the second letter?"

"You are serious," Peecen said, sipping his new drink. "Okay, there's a punch for the first letter-group and another punch in the fifth stop. Fifth letter of the first group is E." He saw that Hank still wasn't satisfied so he held the card up against the light of a lamp advertising beer and read rapidly, "E, W, M, A, N, H, O, W, A, R, D."

It meant nothing to Peecen. Hank stopped holding his breath. "What about the last part of the card?"

"Whatever the programmer wants. It must be a pretty simple code, though. Nothing but 8's straight across. Funny, I thought I knew them all." Peecen was bemused.

"You know all the codes there are?"

"At Monrovia, yeah, at least I thought so. That's where this card comes from. That's where I came from when they fired me."

"You?"

"I ran a programmers' course over there. That bastard keeps getting smarter all the time, and you've got to keep up with him. I mean, the machine, the brain, you know." Peecen said all this as if he were talking about a particularly powerful motor or a good fighter. There was familiarity instead of menace.

"The work you do for Bernhardt must seem pretty simple by comparison."

"Why the hell do you think I'm doing it?" Peecen laughed. "It's boring as hell, though. At least the computer is an interesting bastard. If he wasn't such an egomaniac." He caught Hank's look of surprise. "I mean it. He has tapes filled with nothing but the history of computer development. But what's important to a philosopher like myself is that it's all going into a new language. To him, we're speaking ancient Latin right now. This is a dead language. That's why they have those teaching machines in schools—so that when the kids grow up they'll be able to converse with the computer. Then we'll all be on 9th Street. Won't that be the joke of the century?"

"How smart would you say the computer is?"

124

"How smart would you say a library is?"

"I'd give it an IQ of zero."

"Well, that's what the computer is, an animate library, so I guess that's how smart it is." Peecen took a long drink. "That's what you have to tell yourself anyway."

Peecen lived in a hotel near Hank's and they made it a practice to have a few drinks after work. Hank had learned as much as he could at the public library. He was at that point where lack of practical know-how made more advanced training meaningless. Also, he had a sense of time running out. The day he and Peecen went to the bar the first time the President returned from his vacation. That afternoon, the National Data Center Enabling Act became law.

There was a paradox about the situation that he appreciated. He'd lost his wife, his election, his own name. In return, his life had more shape than ever before. The work in Bernhardt's office gave him a view of society, from the bottom if it came to that, but the vantage point had its compensations. In the libraries he'd studied the history of the computer from the abacus to the Hollerith's electric counting machine in the 1890's to the Defense Department's first true computer in World War II. What Peecen taught him of real technique could tell him even more about his enemy. His life had shape all right, he told himself, as long as he didn't admit the fact that he'd already lost to that enemy, whoever it was.

"It's very simple," Peecen said on the third night. "A digital computer counts digits, like someone counting his fingers if he had millions of them. An analog computer works on the principle of an analogy. Like the instruments of a plane, say. They are part of a computer that registers fuel flow, oil pressure, air pressure, compares them to what the perfect readings should be and adjusts to meet them, to make the readings agree." Hank poured Peecen a drink. It was the price of the course.

"The pilot doesn't take care of all that in a plane?"

"Most of the dials just tell him what the computer is doing. It would take twenty men in the cockpit to do what the computer does."

The analog computer was a vague approximation in comparison to the accuracy of a digital computer, Peecen explained, using fractions to express what a digital computer would define to the last decimal point. And analog computers might react immediately to a new situation, but in advanced digital computers the only speed limit in computation was the speed of light within a micro-transistor.

"Of course, you can't get away from one thing," Peecen said as he reached for the bottle. "Feed the wrong 'perfect reading' into an analog computer and it'll send you out over the Atlantic with a teacup of gas with the most perfect conscience in the world. The pilot will go down wondering why the hell he's dropping, and he'll be dead before he ever figures it out—if he ever would figure out that the plane was in the hands of an insane man who wasn't a man."

"Would a digital computer do that?"

"Sure, that's the point. Give it the wrong information and it'll lie from now to Doomsday. It's just a more sophisticated liar."

"It can tell you what it wants to tell you."

"It can tell you what the man who puts the information in wants to tell you," Peecen corrected. "That's the clearest mark of the superior intelligence, my boy, and we're still the best liars of all."

# CHAPTER THIRTEEN

She saw him walking past the ruins of the Justice Building, a tall, gaunt, faintly bruised man who took long steps. He was dressed in a cheap sports shirt that tried to make him fit in with 9th Street.

"Hank."

He stopped. His legs suddenly felt numb. He turned and saw her. She was running toward him from the corner, her light cotton dress pressed against her front.

"I've been looking all over for you," Daisy said as she caught up.

"Nobody's called me that in a long time."

"I . . . didn't know what else I should call you. Representative Newman would have been a little strange, and I don't know any other names you might have."

"I thought you were back in Iowa with your father."

Daisy made an amateurish shrug of her shoulders. "I'm back. Hamilton Dill wants to talk to you."

"Do you believe who I am?"

"Don't you want to know what he wants?"

"First I want to know what you think. Am I Hank Newman or not?"

She closed her lips on an answer. The expression made her look like a little girl.

"Come on. You must have made up your mind before you tried to find me. Or you wouldn't have tried."

"Okay," she said. "Okay, I think you are."

The public phone on the corner was, strangely, in order. He called Bernhardt to say that he wouldn't be in for the day. "It's a relief," Bernhardt said. "It makes me nervous to work with a saint. Besides, I always knew you whitie boys were shiftless as hell."

"Let's go," Hank said as he hung up. "Have you got a car?"

She nodded.

They drove until they reached MacArthur Drive between Washington and Bethesda. Daisy parked on the shoulder of an exit ramp. They walked through the woods, Hank with his hands in his pockets and Daisy with her arms crossed.

"How did you find me?"

"Kept looking. I've been looking for two weeks. You said that you'd stayed here and I went around to places I thought you might be. I've been on 9th Street a dozen times." She glanced up at the cars on the drive. "We could go to my house. It still isn't sold."

"No, this is better. Did you call Dill?"

"He looked me up when he came to Des Moines."

"Did you discuss my visit with Dill in your home or in his hotel room or on the phone, ever?"

"What has that got to do with it?"

"Well, if you did then we're not alone now." Daisy's pout faded and she rubbed her arms. "Now tell me where you talked."

"We went for a walk after he saw my father. He was only in town for the afternoon."

"Did you call him since?"

"Yes, after he returned to Philadelphia. I called him there. He asked me if I'd had any more visits. We didn't mention your name. You think—"

"Okay. Have you had some other visitors?"

"Agents. You think every phone is bugged? I just saw you make a call."

"It was the normal thing to do if I wasn't going to be there. I told my employer that I planned to get drunk. That's what people in my neighborhood are expected to do."

They sat down on the remains of an old wall. They were cut off in all directions by a ring of hickories and oaks. Not even a shotgun mike could reach them.

"You're so suspicious," she said. "How do you know I'm not bugged?"

"You know me and I think I know you. Now tell me, what did Dill say?"

Her eyes examined the ground at her feet. "He was unhappy about the scene in the tent. He thinks there was something wrong with the computer. He didn't say what, but he was very excited that you still claimed to be innocent."

"Why?"

"It's typical of Dill. He said he made up a programme with all the possibilities for your appearing again with the same story. He ran the programme on a computer he built himself."

"I hate to make a long story short but what was the answer?"

"Apparently the odds were very high that you were either crazy or telling the truth, with an edge to being crazy. I said I didn't think you were." She paused. "By the way, how's your arm?"

"Mostly a shoulder pad wound." He wanted to ask about her father. He had the feeling, though, that she didn't want to talk about him. By coming back to Washington she had, in a sense, betrayed her father, admitted that where he failed someone else might not.

He made a date to see Daisy and Hamilton Dill, and then they drove back to where he could catch a bus. She waved good-bye tentatively, as if she might not see him again. The bus took him to the Washington Mall and he walked from there to 9th Street and

129

Peecen's favorite bar. Hank was into his second drink when the bookkeeper showed up.

"You sneaky bastard, stealing my part when I had my back turned. We're very bad influences on each other, Mr. Poster. I've taken to work and you've taken to drink. Now I'll have to work twice as hard to catch up. A double, please, barkeep."

"Some calls for you, professor," the bartender said as he slid the glass over.

"Good. Tear them up." He turned to Hank. "You should see Bernhardt. Happy as a tick. Going around telling everybody you were out in the gutter. Frankly, I'm disappointed not to find you better greased. You look almost sober, bite my tongue."

They went to Hank's room later. He didn't trust Peecen's anymore. In his own, he could make a quick check of the small signs he'd left to tell him whether someone else had come in during the day—a match balanced on a bureau drawer, powder on the underside of a doorknob, a bit of putty in a crack of the floor just inside the room. They were all undisturbed.

"What I don't understand," Hank said, "is why an immense operation like the data center would use punched cards. You say that's the most primitive input/output tool there is."

"Who changed the subject to computers? God, my throat is dry." Hank took the bottle out from under the bed. "Ah, you were asking about the cards. Well, thank you, it's true that 99 percent of storage in something as complicated as the Monrovia computer is done on those new laser tapes. Wicked to see those little bastards spinning and know that Shakespeare goes by in a millisecond. But cards are still used sometimes for operations that are very low volume and that don't need much speed. I wasn't too involved in that part of the complex. We geniuses are the plebeians at Monrovia." He added a complicated curse.

"Who was in charge?"

"There are some administrators. Of course, saying that they run the computer is like saying a flea on the back of an elephant could tell him where to go."

Fleas. Elephants. Peecen smiled from Hank's memory. He stood on the boardwalk and looked out on the ocean. It was two days later, a Saturday, the day he was meeting Dill and Daisy Hansen. There wasn't much company on the boardwalk, just some pensioners too poor to leave Atlantic City. They set up beach chairs on the boards and, staring at the dark surf pounding onto the black beach, hugged sweaters against the gray wind. Not many vacationers came to Atlantic City anymore, not since the tanker disaster a year before when two Japanese ships collided off the New Jersey coast and released a couple of million gallons of low-grade oil. The Miss America contest moved to Miami.

Hank chewed on a piece of saltwater taffy. It tasted more of ocean than the air did. There was an angry reek to it, just as the waves slammed futilely on clotted sand.

He saw two figures moving along the planks laid down on the beach. He walked down the steps, passing a sign that said, "No Running, Playing Ball, Pets, Alcoholic Beverages, Litter." It was the cleanest thing on the beach.

Dill shouted into the wind. "This is a hell of a place to meet. Notice? No birds."

Dill was right. There wasn't a gull in the sky. The wind almost knocked them off the planks. There had been a storm at sea.

"Can't we go someplace to talk?" Daisy said. "We can hardly hear each other."

"That's why this is a good place to talk."

131

"Daisy tells me you're going in for the cloak-and-dagger routine."

"Can you give me a reason why I shouldn't? Did you bring the papers I asked for?"

"Yeah," Dill said. His hair was longer than Daisy's and it kept blowing over his eyes. He squinted through it at Hank. "Yeah."

"Come on, we'd better keep walking," Hank said.

As they walked, the planks sank with wet noises into the pitch underneath. Clouds skudded close overhead to the city.

"This is nutty but everything's nutty," Dill said. "It was weird. I've been around computers ever since I was a kid. That night at the cemetery it was like hearing your father was Hitler. First the computer hesitated giving an answer. That's not something a machine does. Then, and this is really incredible, it lied. Not an out and out lie. The guy asked for a report on Arthur Jameson right after questions about yours and the dead man's fingerprints. By strict logic, the computer is compelled to give a report on Jameson's fingerprints. Instead, it gave another report, a report pertinent to the subject of Jameson but absolutely not the answer logically called for. It should have given the fingerprints and only then a further report on Jameson's status."

"Why was the Assistant Director happy then?" Daisy asked.

"Because in his mind the real question always is whether the Bureau's name is in trouble," Hank answered. "If the Bureau had conveniently caught Jameson hours before, then Jameson could no longer be involved, period. Checking prints after that information was disclosed would be an insult to the competence of the Bureau, right, Mr. Dill? It was a perfect answer, attuned to the psychology of the person ask-

132

ing the question, and avoided another odd wave of arson like the one about my own prints."

"You're not crazy," Dill said.

"Thank you."

"It proves what I feared. Remember that voice you told us about, the one on the phone after the shooting? That must have been one of the men involved in this"—he fumbled for words—"amazing conspiracy. That was a man on the phone, and I tell you that was a man on the other end of that relay at the cemetery. See what I'm getting at? It was a fake. The whole Monrovia setup is a power grab by men who are pretending to be a computer."

They stopped talking and forced themselves to walk again. Daisy took one arm of each.

"It's so simple. All that information is only going to Monrovia because it will be in the hands of an impersonal machine incapable of ambition or deceit. If it isn't a machine, then you've given whoever gets that secret data a gun against the head of every person in the country from the President on down."

"It's a pretty wild conclusion," Daisy said. Hank was silent.

"It's the only logical one, the only one I can come to. The transmission from the panel in the tent to the computer was set on the microwave band approved for Monrovia by the FCC. It was never off it during the whole time, which means that we had to be talking to Monrovia. But we can't know whether we weren't just talking to men there."

"There is a computer there, though, I know that," Hank said.

"Yes, to hold all the information they want. Obviously, they can cut in when they want to right from inside the complex itself."

"But you asked some questions at the panel before all that began."

133

"They trapped me like a baby. With an encyclopedic computer like that, you often ask it to fill in random quotations just to check the speed. Every machine has its quirks. A car does and so does a computer. I'd heard that the Monrovia computer had a taste for Germans. The big ones are filled with Boolean logic, Kantian philosophy and so on. It's just a matter of giving them enough relays and the training to use them. Don't get excited, there's nothing so peculiar about it, in fact, it's most a matter of which relays are the best designed. The master computer at Monrovia was programmed to do a new translation of *Thus Spake Zarathustra*, and I opted for a line from that. Whoever was on the other end was ready to handle me as he was for the old man from the Bureau."

"And Celia," Daisy said. "My father gave me a reason why she might have broken down on the phone. He knew her when she was just starting out, when she was married. She accidentally killed her husband, ran him down in a driveway one night. The whole thing was hushed up. Everyone knew he drank too much and practically walked into the car. The only place the information could be found is at Monrovia, according to Dad." She ducked her head into the wind. "I can't think of anything else that would scare Celia except a threat to open the case again. They must be very vicious men."

They came to the end of the planks. There was nothing more but dark, gritty beach. The shell of a horseshoe crab had the dull glow of a piece of coal. They turned and started back.

"There's something else then," Dill said. "The computer can't be vicious. It has an Ethic."

They looked at him.

"It's an offshoot of the space exploration. NASA had a special computer built for the Earth-to-Jupiter shot. The thing is a thousand times more exciting than putting a man on the moon. Consider a brain traveling to every planet in the solar system between us and Jupiter and sending the information back. It's very tricky work, programming a computer for something like that, because you don't know what to programme it for. You don't know what's out there to begin with. Then, there's that mass of new information coming in. They decided that even a computer would become confused by the flow unless it was related by the programmers to some general rule or goal. They called it the Ethic, what the computer would use as its general order. It's very difficult to explain to laymen because I have to simplify things so much, and what I'm really talking about is an interaction of transistorized circuitry."

"And the master computer at Monrovia has an Ethic, too?"

"Right. You'll find it in the papers." Dill slapped his windbreaker. "The idea was to find the most general, most innocuous guide, especially after they conceived the idea of using the computer complex for reorganizing government bureacracies. Actually, designers were so careful they made the Ethic in two parts. I was able to get hold of it only because the Institute was involved in the research."

Dill stopped talking as a helicopter passed overhead. It came to a halt about a hundred yards out over the water. They watched as a passenger in the 'copter lowered a container into the waves. The wind tugged at the container as it came back up with its sample, spilling most of it before it got back to the men inside.

"Just no birds," Hank said.

"Two parts," Dill went on. "First, 'No input will be accepted, no programme run or output rendered that is detrimental to the benefit or best interests of the United States of America.'"

135

"The second part?"

"That 'No order will supercede this Ethic.' That's what I've been trying to tell you all along. The computer is honest; it couldn't lie if it wanted to. When they used it to lie about you, they as much as said the computer wasn't talking and they were."

They reached the stairs to the boardwalk.

"I don't see how we're any further than we were before," Daisy said.

"It took two million years for man to evolve and thirty years for the computer. You've got to give us more than an afternoon," Hank said.

"At least, we know who our enemy isn't," Dill said.

# CHAPTER FOURTEEN

"Mr. Poster?"

"Yes." Hank felt a small electric charge go down his back. Bernhardt was busy at his desk stamping plane tickets.

"We haven't spoken in some time."

He tried guessing the accent. It was the third time he'd heard the voice and he could distinguish it from a million others; he'd know it till the day he died. Midwestern. Flat. Soft. Not from the Corn Belt.

"You are free to talk, aren't you, Mr. Poster?"

"Usually, you do all the talking."

"True enough." Again there was a space for a laugh that didn't come. "How are things? Are you happy?"

"I'm making do."

"Good, that's the American spirit. Everyone's very impressed at the way you've managed. Are you free for lunch today?"

"I haven't got anything on my calendar that's too important."

"Great. I was wondering if you'd like to pop in and see me?"

"Sure." He forced his voice to keep from breaking. "Where is your office? I'd better tell the boss if it's far away."

"Not far at all. In fact, just across the street. Ask the construction foreman for Room 10-B. He'll tell you where to go. Let's say 12:30."

137

"I'll be there," Hank said. The line was dead. He put the receiver down.

Across the street? Hank went to the window. There was nothing across the street but condemned houses until the Justice Building. A truck rolled out of the building's bottom floor with a load of concrete dust. They had started work again.

At 12:25 Hank was at the Justice Building gate. A guard cleared him with a phone call. Inside, he could see how big the building was. The trucks carted debris out of shafts that reached fifty feet below ground level. The concrete pillars that had withstood the bombs were fifteen stories of broken light and shadow. A few bare light bulbs provided sparse blazes in the labyrinth. A heavy man with a hardhat stood beside the truck road with a walkie-talkie. He told Hank to follow the road to the second shaft and take the elevator there to the tenth floor.

The elevator was nothing but a wire cage. It rose within the greater cage of bare beams and pre-cast slabs. He considered the possibility that the elevator might just take a fast plunge to the bottom of the building's foundation and dismissed it. To think he was still so dangerous was egotistic. The cage stopped and he opened the wire door.

He was on what appeared to be an average executive suite floor. The floor was thickly carpeted, and indirect fixtures lit the ceiling. On one wall was a print of 18th century Washington. Still, it seemed deserted. The carpet was too new. His feet left the only marks on it. He found 10-B at the end of the hall. The door was open.

Nobody was inside. The office was luxuriously finished with the same deep carpet, a large rosewood desk, leather chairs, wide, antiqued mirrors and a view through vertical louvers of the Capitol Building five miles away. There was a tray on the desk. On the tray was a plate of roast beef and potatoes, a salad, bread and butter, a tall glass of iced tea and a short one of scotch. The food was warm and the drinks were cold. A phone on the desk rang.

"Mr. Poster. I'm sorry I couldn't make it down. We'll just have to make do with the phone again, I'm afraid. Anyway, I didn't want to cheat you of your lunchtime. There is a lunch there, isn't there?"

"Yes."

"Fine. Just set the phone in the cradle of the intercom, and we can talk without your holding it. That's it."

The voice came from speakers in each corner of the room when Hank put the phone down as he was directed.

"I hope you're not too disappointed. I ordered your favorite lunch, though. Go ahead, I don't mind if you eat while we talk."

Hank pulled a chair up to the desk. Besides the phone, the intercom and the tray, it was bare.

"You must have just moved in," Hank said.

"Why do you say that?"

"You haven't even had time to put a picture of your wife here." He cut the meat. It was rare, the way he liked it.

"I'm not married, like you. Speaking of moving, though, some of us were surprised that you hadn't gone someplace else. To start afresh in new surroundings. A man with your ability to adjust would have had no trouble rising in a small town."

"Well, you know the saying, how you gonna keep them down on the farm?"

"You've made a satisfactory life for yourself here?"

"No complaints. Oh, I'm not saying that I'm not a little bitter. To be bitter is human and all that. I don't see any point in trying to hide, if that's what you're driving at. I know I couldn't."

"Go on."

"Well, who knows, maybe I can be of more use to you. Not as a dupe next time but as a regular employee. Don't you think you owe it to me?"

"What could you possibly do for us?"

"I don't know. I thought you might have an idea." He slid the fork through the potato.

"Mr. Poster, Mr. Poster, I will start getting ideas only when you do. I am confident that you will not, if you understand what I mean."

Hank shrugged and stood up. "There's another old saying. Hope springs."

"Eternal," the voice said when Hank didn't.

Hank listened to the whirr of the elevator on the way down. It had been close in the room; he'd said almost too much. He knew how they'd used the phone to keep tabs on him and listed to all the maneuverings of Senator Hansen and Perafini. It was in the Congressional Record Hansen showed him. The computerized voice graph that singled out voices like fingerprints so that the public would be protected from official eavesdropping. Whenever or wherever he used a phone, his own voice would give him away and trigger a tape. He thought it would be safe to mention it as the observation of a casualty until he thought about the mirrors.

The voice could have dealt with him on the phone in Bernhardt's office. The only reason for inviting him into the Justice Building was for someone else to get a good look at him. He knew it wasn't the voice. The voice would have noticed that he never ate a bite or drank, although he did shove the food around his plate. They were still interested in him, curious because there were one or two days they couldn't account for. Right now, the voice—he decided it was more Southwestern—was thinking about the last exchange and deciding it was a joke. He hoped.

The elevator landed with a jolt. He got out and followed a truck out of the building. The foreman was still posted outside.

"So they're finally going to use this place," Hank said.

"If it don't collapse, why not? You should see the cracks in the foundation. You're not going to find me in there."

"I wish you'd told me before I went in."

"You went in to see Mr. Monroe, so I figured you knew what you were doing."

Hank paused to light a cigaret and offer the foreman one. "He's some guy. I never did find out what the first initial stood for."

"James," the foreman said after a frown of thought. "That's what the requisition slip said. James Monroe."

Hank went through the gate and walked back to Bernhardt's. He was hungry but satisfied. The voice had a name, at last.

He spent the afternoon chartering a plane for a Venezuelan soccer team, finding an old client for his parole officer and handling the negotiations between Bernhardt and a local police captain. The charges clients were booked on had a direct result on the bails demanded, and captains had a great deal of leeway on what the charges would be. At 6 o'clock, he was bushed. He turned down Peecen's invitation to warm a bar stool.

She was waiting for him in her car. When she called out, he kept on walking.

"Hank, what's the matter?" Daisy's car followed him as he went around the nearest corner away from the Justice Building.

"What's going on?" she asked again when he jumped in beside her.

"They're watching from the Justice Building."

"It's abandoned."

141

"Not anymore. I was there today. I met them."

"How?" She had so many questions she didn't know what to ask.

"He asked me to, the man on the phone. I didn't see him actually. His office was empty, but I talked to him over the intercom. I think it was just to look me over. But it's getting dangerous now."

"He threatened you?"

"Vaguely. It was more to remind me of my place. I'm not going to fool them forever."

Daisy started the car. It was an old Thunderbird, and she was proud of the way she handled the stick shift, but her main motive was to get moving. He watched stonily through the windshield.

"What do you want me to do?"

"I think it's time you got lost. Literally." He felt her glancing at him. "Go back to Des Moines."

They drove on for a long time before she spoke again.

"What are you going to do? Carry on 'the good fight'? You've been bucking for martyr from the beginning."

"It's my privilege."

"And I'm supposed to play the weak sex, slinking off when things start happening? It isn't a football game, you know. You don't have to weigh 200 pounds for politics."

"I don't think this is politics and it's not your being a girl."

"When you're over twenty-one people call you a woman. At least, some people do."

"Pardon me."

They went on for another mile in silence. Hank became uneasy. The neighborhood was new to him and, more than that, he was afraid of being seen in her car. He should never have come.

"Your father would be happier if you got out of this."

"My father isn't here, as you once said. You are and I am. And Dill," she added.

"I want both you and Dill out of it."

"So this is real life and only heroes can play. You're very selfish."

Hank let a small smile get to his face. "And here I thought I was being noble."

"Tough. You're not going to be noble with me."

He saw where they were. Daisy had approached her house from a new angle. She parked in front of it.

"Are you crazy?"

"That was my line the last time you were here. I guess things have changed."

A black sedan parked fifty yards behind them. Hank looked in the rear-view mirror. Two men were sitting in it with nothing to do. Daisy looked into the mirror. He had to give her credit. Her cheeks lost their color for only a second.

"Now there's no backing out. I might as well make you a decent supper."

Hank swore as he shut the car door. The For Sale sign was down. She was committing herself on a grand scale.

Daisy busied herself to the point of parody getting a meal together. He had the feeling he was supposed to be ashamed of relegating her to the kitchen, so he deliberately wandered around the living room. Some of the pictures were back up, and there were a couple dozen books practically lost in the vast bookcases. One of them was a political biography of her father called *Profile of an Independent Man. There have been a thousand descriptions and symbols of independence*, Hank read. *They're usually of bloody heroes or vainglorious politicians. The one that always comes to my mind is a strip of concrete buckled and*

143

*broken open by a single, indomitable blade of grass.
It is a constant reminder that Nature abhors tyranny
just as much as She abhors a vacuum.* It was a quote
from Everett Hansen. Hank put the book back on the
shelf.

The supper was a salad of sardines.

"I'd planned on antipasto, but I couldn't find the
anchovies."

They talked about the book on her father. Daisy
asked him whether he read much.

"As a kid. My father brought me up on Jack London, Kipling, even Homer. I loved the stories about
the Trojan War. Then the older I got the less I liked
it."

"You didn't like studying?"

"It seemed I couldn't pick up a book without feeling that I was pumping up some writer's ego. The
personality got between me and the story. People use
their jobs to fulfill their egos. Doctors, bankers, politicians, sergeants."

"Maybe you stopped reading because you didn't
want to communicate."

"That's true enough, I didn't. Not that way, anyway. Or maybe I felt I wasn't going to get that much
out of it, just reading for no reason except to show I
could."

"You've been waiting for a reason?"

"I guess so." His eye fell on the kitchen window sill.
A copy of *Profile of an Independent Man* lay against
the sash. "You have a good enough reason to read
that."

"Uh huh. You probably didn't notice before because Dad wanted them hidden, but I have a copy in
every room. I'm very proud of him."

"You should be." He said it before he thought about
it. He was thankful that he had because the inflection

of his voice would have changed. "I'll have to get you the Gideon Bible sometime."

He wrote on a piece of paper and passed it to her, then he got a knife out of the drawer. Daisy was mystified, but she went on prattling about her father's early career as a New Deal Congressman. Hank took the book from the sill, put it on the table and cut along the binding inside the front cover. The physical attributes of the book limited the nature of a possible bug and he was only presuming. He stopped presuming when he peeled the paper off the inside of the cover. Set flush with the cardboard was a small metal plate. He showed it to Daisy. Fortunately she was between sentences because she threw her hand over her mouth. He let the plate lie where it was.

"I've got these sardines all over my shirt now."

"It'll come out. I'll show you."

They went into the bathroom. Hank turned both faucets on full blast.

"Haven't got one of the books in here, have you?"

Daisy shook her head. "God, how long has it been there?"

"Have. There's one in every book, I'm sure. I don't know how long."

"Maybe we could turn their power off?"

"No power to turn off. They're simply resonators. They bounce an FM beam off them with shotgun transmitters. The beam goes back disturbed by the plate reacting to our voices. The safest bug of all. Besides, fooling with the plates would be the most suspicious thing we could do. As soon as we get downstairs, you'll have to find me some glue and we'll paste the paper back."

"That's not good enough." Daisy's mind had skipped ahead of his.

"What's wrong with that?"

"They're already suspicious. That thing is in the

book. They saw you come in here. They'll want to know why."

"I think that's pretty obvious. It's also obvious that the sooner I clear out of here the better."

"That's the worst thing you can do. What do they know? You're here with me. We didn't say anything that said why. If they don't have another explanation, of course, they'd end up with the idea that we're talking about them. There are other reasons for a man and a woman being alone in a house, though."

It took a while to dawn on him. He groaned and reached for the door.

"I'm not a good enough reason?"

"That's not it and you know it. It just wouldn't work and it would get you more involved."

"I'm already involved, and who knows if it'll work if we don't try it?"

His hand stayed on the doorknob. She applied the clinching argument.

"Remember, the only reason I'm sure you're really Hank Newman is that I dislike you so much. I don't think either of us would get carried away."

A minute later when they came out, Daisy was giggling. "Stop it. I just said I was going to wash your shirt, not you."

"Then give the shirt back to me." His shirt was on his back. He lit a cigaret and gave her one.

"I'm not getting within ten feet of you," Daisy said with a squeal that had nothing to do with the seriousness on her face.

"I've got you now," Hank said. He wanted to see how she would squirm out of that.

"Mmmmmmmmmmm. I like it."

He turned on his heel and walked into the living room. She kept up with him.

"You're so forceful."

"You're such a lousy liar," Hank mouthed silently.

146

"It's about time for me to go," he said aloud. "You know how I hate to."

"Don't then. I didn't bring you here to have supper." She scribbled madly on a pad, *Don't be so difficult. Nobody'd believe you just came here for sardines.* "I wish you wouldn't tease me like this."

"If you insist. Then I think I'll get a drink. I could use one," he said with emphasis.

"So could I."

They passed the time playing records, reading each other's notes and uttering occasional pleasantries. Hank found himself getting angrier as time went on. The whole thing was a bad joke. Seeing him angry made Daisy just as mad.

*For a while you had me thinking it did matter if Howard Newman was alive. I'm going to bed.*

She heard the note being torn up as she climbed the stairs.

Hank sat and stared gloomily at his drink. It was too late to go back now. The buses had stopped running. Besides, the whole stupid fraud would fall apart if he left, he thought.

He found her in the bathroom filing her nails. He turned the faucets on. "It's not as simple as that, Miss Hansen. You thought up this idea and there's one last touch you have to put on it."

"What's that?" She pulled her bathrobe around herself.

"Is there a book in your bedroom?"

"Yes. Oh no! Forget it."

"Don't be silly, of course not. I'll sleep on the couch downstairs. But our voices have to be heard in the bedroom. You don't like it and I don't like it, but the men listening damn well expect something."

"I could have stabbed you with the scissors once. I can use this now." She held the file point at him.

147

"Stop being a baby." He turned the faucets off and opened the door. "Come on."

They went down the hall, Hank leading the way. He opened the bedroom door and stepped in. Daisy hesitated at the door, between the dark of the room and the light in the hall. Her body was erotically silhouetted within the robe. He looked away.

"Come on."

She shook her head.

"Come on," he said more urgently.

"Whatever you say . . . dear," she said tensely.

That was enough for Hank. He tried to walk past her into the hall when he felt a scratch in his side. She'd tried to stab him again.

"Are you out of your mind?" he whispered. "Give that to me."

She slashed at his arm and he grabbed her wrist. "Let go or I'll kill you," she whispered hoarsely.

"You'll try harder if I let go," he said into her ear.

She tried to knee him and they fell to the floor. Daisy was under him, trying frantically to get away. It was something that had nothing to do with him, but he could feel more than the file between them. He rolled off, still holding onto her wrist. In the half-light from the hall, her eyes were translucent and large. The tinny sound of the file dropping on the floor pierced their strained breathing.

Daisy rolled toward him instead of away. Her long legs touched his. Her fingers touched his eyebrow as her hips and the hard mound between them grazed his pants. The close-fitting top of her robe pressed her breasts together. He offered no explanation as he kissed her. Her eyes closed as she pulled his face down for a second, longer kiss.

Her mouth opened wide to take his and her hips pushed into his. He slipped the shoulder of her robe back, exposing one breast. It was white, so white that the veins on its shadow made it appear almost blue. Its nipple was pink and erect. He'd made love with other women, but none of them had been particularly friends or enemies before they'd gone to bed. Knowing Daisy the way he did gave the bare breast a powerful, touching worth. He kissed it and the nipple grew harder and darker.

"Do you think they're listening?" she asked with a calm smile.

"Let them suffer."

Her hand fumbled with his fly. He opened it for her and she drew out the stiff organ. She held it as if she were protecting it.

"Thank God, I'm not a virgin. No, not the bed, please, Hank. I can't stand the idea of them hearing the bedsprings. I want to enjoy it."

He undid the knot of her robe and she raised her hips so that he could draw her pants off. She lay on the robe, naked, her arms back so that her hands were in the hall, while he undressed.

"How do you keep in shape?"

"Running."

Her breasts became rounder as she put her arms up for him. The blond curls of her Venus mound turned the light from the hall into gold coils. Her long legs spread as he lay down on her. He was in her before their lips met. She raised her hips more, and he penetrated the full length. Daisy pulled his head into her neck and rubbed her cheek into his hair. She had been ready all the time.

"Nothing like taking a book to bed," she whispered.

# CHAPTER FIFTEEN

"I've never hated anyone so much in my life. I knew there had to be a good reason," Daisy said. "Besides, it does fit into our alibi. Maybe they'll think we're on a honeymoon."

"The computer registers all marriage licenses."

"How romantic."

The veil of water, a blue and gray wall, fell into the mist, then rose from the water's own destruction, except that it reshaped itself as a tame and placid lake. A small tug, *The Maid of the Mist*, dodged intrepidly through the rocks. They watched from a platform that ran down the Canadian side of the falls. From time to time the mists rose and covered them like a low-flying cloud. Daisy's words dissolved into the roar of the tons of water plunging into space.

Their motel was only a hundred feet away. Perafini had chosen the Niagara Quality Cascade because of its proximity to the falls. Even with the windows closed, it sounded as though the tide was about to come in. The blinds of Cabin 14 moved as Hank and Daisy approached and the door opened for them.

Perafini and Dill were still arguing.

"These are men with top security clearances. I supervised some of the reviews myself. Besides, they're all from different parties, ideologies, not the sort of men who'd band together for a conspiracy."

"Hank was told to use the Justice Building."

"Not even the Justice Department has that many

traitors," Perafini said sarcastically. Since the episode at Arlington, Perafini had been shunted to advisor to the intelligence bureau of the Royal Canadian Mounted Police in Ottawa. Dill had made contact with him at Hank's request. Hank wondered if they always carried on like this or whether the grind of the last thirty-six hours was getting to them. The chairs and beds were covered with papers so the two men were standing.

"Here's your coffee. Sorry we took so long," Daisy said. She handed them their black and cream-no-sugar and then took one to the newcomer, a kid with beard and beads who made Dill look as straight as Dagwood. "It sounds like you need a break, too."

"We just had one, an emotional break," Perafini said. "It's good for the nerves."

"Hank's the one taking the chance," Dill said.

"You've got it backwards," Hank said. "I've got nothing to lose, everything to gain. Al, this would really be the end of your career if they found out how you set this up. Dill, I think the Institute would find some reason for terminating your contract. And Emory? What would they do?"

"The Canadians would send me back if they were pushed hard enough." Emory Kristopis-Paine smiled as if he would be amazed by any other result. "Being a deserter from the U.S. Army doesn't automatically make you popular here. Then, too, I'm a homosexual and they could trump up something. My father would be very angry if they didn't."

Just the sight of Emory had put Hank off at the beginning. Dill explained the slight young man was essential, just as his father Konstantine Kristopis-Paine, mentor of the Hudson Institute, was essential to formulation of the U.S. war game psychology. The son was not strictly speaking a scientist but, by raining

151

a scientific historian. He was an offshoot of the new conscience of the scientific community that had emerged after the creation of the Atom Bomb, exploded at Hiroshima five years before he was born. Trained in all the physical sciences, he used his knowledge to study the evolution of scientific thought. In the past day and a half, Hank had found his the steadiest, most active mind of all.

"It'll be worth it," Emory said. "This is the most amazing collection of records I've ever seen." He patted the pile of transcripts on his lap.

"But the important thing is Monrovia now, not some meeting ten years ago," Dill said. Dill had insisted they include Emory because, as he said, scientists tend to be as ignorant as ostriches when it comes to the world outside their own private laboratory. Emory would provide the perspective of the scientific historian, but at the moment Dill was impatient with perspective.

"Our way out of this mess is to enlist the computer on our side. We know there are men at Monrovia subverting the computer for their own ends. If we can only discover how they've created their bypass in the circuitry and reconnect the computer, its Ethic will help us to expose those men. It's a case of technology, pure and simple," Dill concluded.

"I have to agree," Perafini said. "We've been over the other angles and we're generally in accord from what you've told us, Hank, that Duggs and Fien and the President and everybody else in Washington has not gone mad or evil. Men from every ideological stripe are involved. Many with the highest security clearance, some of them I've reviewed myself. I'd be willing to grant that some of them may be operating deliberately for some sort of political coup, but I think the real enemy, as I understand it, is using a technological tactic. Get the men in Monrovia and

152

you attack the leaders. Get Duggs or Fien and there are a hundred other proponents of the data center to take their places."

"Damn," Dill said, "I've been getting through. That's what I've been yelling all this time. It's a technological problem. Don't you think so, Hank?"

"The problem lies not in our technology but in ourselves," Emory said. Dill glanced at him angrily.

"What do you think, Hank?"

Hank did not betray his amusement at the thought that there had been a time when Dill didn't think he should have an opinion. "I think I'd like to hear more about the computer itself. You said it was a hybrid computer, neither analog nor digital."

"With the advantages of both, absolutely accurate and capable of simultaneous reaction to changing situations. It's also called an open-ended brain because its design is sophisticated enough to assimilate new information on its own without requiring new hardware or programming."

Hank shuffled some papers around. "You told me it was a baby of the Space Computer."

"That's right. The Jupiter brain. Scientists at NASA recognized that we don't know everything there is in space and that no amount of programming, even laser tapes, could handle a situation that we couldn't even imagine existed before the computer's satellite ran into it. Imagine, a payload full of memory chips taking man's place where he can't go."

"That's almost as romantic as the bit about the marriage licenses," Daisy said.

"It is romantic in its way," Hank said. "The 1st Generation computer of thermionic valves begat the 2nd Generation computer of transistors which begat the 3rd Generation computers of integrated memory circuit chips. The end result: one mammoth, moronic slave."

"I don't know if I'm supposed to be reassured or not," Daisy said. "I think I will be, since we're superior. There is a difference between our intelligence and its, isn't there?" she asked Emory.

"That's like asking if there's a definite difference between plant life and animal life. People draw the lines at different places. Tell them about the three lobes, Hamilton."

"Now that's a simplification," Dill said. "What actually happened is that there is a separation of the Jupiter brain into three parts. This way the space agency guards against mistakes. If one section of the computer makes an analysis that the other two parts disagree with, they can override it." As he became more nervous, he talked with his hands. "The three parts are called the Id, the Ego and the Superego."

The sound of the falls swelled in the silence that followed.

"I'm sorry; that is a little chilling," Daisy said.

"What else did you expect them to pattern a mechanical brain after?" Emory asked. "We have the only model there is."

"And what is the difference, that we're flesh and blood?"

"Oh no," Dill jumped in, "that makes no difference at all. Our brains are just electric circuitry, too."

"The fact is," Emory said, "human brains are better than the best computers. You can't calculate as fast, you can't bring forth items from your memory banks as regularly. But there is an interweaving of cells in your brain that makes the average computer's circuits look like a pile of children's blocks. You can relate memories and concepts and sensations to a practically unlimited degree. What you have is so good there's no decent explanation for it."

"Thank you, Emory. I'm glad someone had a good word for the home team."

"A master computer with three lobes then," Hank said. "It controls the computer complex. Who controls the master, we don't know. Assuming someone does."

"We are assuming that," Perafini said. "Remember what you told us about that room in the Justice Building. You heard a sound you recognized as the sound of a generator."

"It wasn't the elevator. I'm sure of that."

"And there were men watching you from behind the mirrors. The association is pretty clear. Those men had access to a Monrovia relay run by that generator. It's time to get those men before they get us. One fast move."

"On Monrovia, you mean. A commando raid?"

"Why not? Except in this case it'll be me and a few of my old friends, plus some experts who can correct the bypass. As long as they're not suspecting us, it shouldn't be too difficult. Monrovia isn't Cuba."

"I don't like it. You don't know anything about the place. There is a security force."

"Not much," Dill said. "I've never been there, but I can tell you that there's not much point in trying to rob a computer complex. Computers are too heavy to steal and besides, a thief would have to be an expert to go undetected for more than minute. In Federal data banks with confidential information, at least two employees have to witness the transfer of any tapes."

"At night?" Perafini suggested.

"They work twenty-four hours a day. The important thing is to know where to go and what to do. For example, part of the relay communications come into the complex by military cable and part of them come by microwave transmission. I can identify the receivers for you." Dill paused because he was going to use a simile he didn't like. "The data channels are the computer's senses, without them it knows nothing.

155

Once we find the data receiving rooms we'll find the men, because that's where the bypass has to be."

"How much damage would we do if there's any shooting?"

Emory supplied the answer. "Like the human brain, the computer feels no pain."

"I don't like it," Hank said.

"Why?" Perafini asked.

"I'd like to. I'd like to get my hands on somebody, really. But it just doesn't feel right. You're jumping into this blind."

"I can get a complete floorplan of the Monrovia complex. We drop on the roof itself. How dangerous can it be? Like raiding the library."

"That's not what I meant. Look, the only real contact you people have had with the enemy is me. I was the Monrovia candidate, remember? I was in the shower. I was the one who talked to him on the phone, three times. I was in his office. And I don't feel this is right."

"You did feel you were dealing with a man," Emory said.

Dill raised his eyes to the ceiling but Hank answered seriously.

"Yes. A strange, cold man. Intelligent and confident, very confident."

"Did you think he was just a spokesman?"

"I felt there were others. He mentioned others and I believed him. But he wasn't just a spokesman."

"As soon as we expose his use of the computer to monitor phone calls of Senators, he's done for," Perafini said. Only Dill and Daisy heard him.

"There are some items in these papers Dill stole for you," Emory said. "Some of them you marked."

"Things I was curious about," Hank said.

"So am I. Here on page 102 of the Buck Hill Falls Conference attended by liberal and left-wing members of Congress and scientists in 1968. In a speech by a Dr. Harnick of Columbia, he says that 'Russia is now developing a nationwide computer network around its powerful new RJAD. This network will be designed to cooperate with similar networks in other Warsaw Pact nations. The advanced RJAD is similar to the most sophisticated American computer and represents a great leap forward for Soviet technology.' I'm skipping. 'The ideal is that both great nations, the United States and the Soviet Socialist Republics, will employ their computers for the mutual benefit of man, not only in national industrial and social planning but also in the field of national relations. Whereas we have yet to succeed in writing a treaty in English and Russian, would it not be inevitable that two objective, dispassionate computers should do so in Fortran, the new international computer language?' "

"What's all that about?" Perafini asked.

"Emory and I are wondering why some politicians who usually jump and holler at Big Brother tactics were so overjoyed over the data center. Tell me this: Is it conceivable that someone with that dream would ask the computer whether it was inevitable?"

"It is equipped to formulate government planning, which is dependent on just such predictions. It shouldn't have given an answer but it could. In odds, of course. Like, 6-1 on Peace, 100-1 on Bliss. The trouble is that it would have given the same answer to right-wingers who'd think a treaty with the Reds is like getting caught with syph."

"Okay," Hank said, although he wasn't satisfied. "You mentioned some other items."

"Yes." Emory snatched a new piece of paper. "Transcript from the Miami Symposium in 1967. It was supposed to be a group from the American Medical Association but in fact it was a 'think tank' congress to

157

discuss Defense Department programs. I notice that the classification of this record has been moved up from CONFIDENTIAL to SECRET. Anyway, there was an odd speech given to the circle on cybernetics by an anthropologist, a Professor Francisco Wolf from Southern California.

"'Recent evidence suggests that we will have to rethink our previous concepts of man as a scavenger and of his opposable thumb as the mainspring to the evolution of tool-making and intelligence. Findings in Zambia suggest that man was a hunter rather than a gatherer of berries who fought wild dogs for the carcasses of the kills of predators. Man was the predator, probably the most successful one in his realm. There is evidence that during this period as a predator his brain capacity quadrupled and his tool-making developed as part of his endeavor to catch game faster and with less danger to himself. General evidence from a variety of anthropological and zoological sources shows that the predator is invariably and by necessity more intelligent than the prey it catches. Living off inanimate plant life produces a static, docile mentality. Living off live, elusive forms produces an active, adaptive, inventive mentality that must outwit its adversary or die. This is the most brutal form of natural selection and the most effective. The hunter is smarter.'

"That's all. The comments of his audience have been deleted."

"That's some speech to make to a group of computer analysts," Dill said. "Maybe they didn't say anything."

"I think they did," Hank said.

"Why?" Daisy asked.

"I've seen the hunter."

158

# CHAPTER SIXTEEN

Hank tried to concentrate on the forms Peecen drew on the paper. The square stood for PROCESSING. The rhomboid was INPUT/OUTPUT. A four-sided figure with one short side represented MANUAL KEYBOARD. A Q-like figure meant MAGNETIC TAPE. There were a dozen more esoteric symbols.

"This is how you design a flowchart. You don't need one word. The bosses there even use numbers for the VIPs. If you're from the Pentagon, you're CODE 4. If you're from Congress, you're CODE 5. At least, that's what the programmers tell me."

Peecen dipped the bottle's neck into the glass.

"You're not even listening. Am I getting this for free?"

"Sorry, my mind wandered. You were saying about codes."

"Nothing much, I don't know what the codes stand for, they're so vague. Maybe they should use the seven ages of man. 'One man in his time plays many parts. At first the infant, mewling and puking in the nurse's arms.' Ah, nobody appreciates a literary background."

Hank was staring out the window again. He was thinking of what Emory had told them in the motel, about MASSSTER.

The Army happily drafted Emory in 1970. He was the heir of the Kristopis-Paine expertise in computers and they could use him. He was shipped to Fort Hood, Texas, to work in a $70 million Defense Department project. Although he had no rating, he was

159

giving orders to captains and majors. The Army wanted a battlefield computer. Its test name was Mobile Army Surround Sensor System, Evaluation and Review. MASSSTER. What the Pentagon wanted was a computer system that could be responsible for a given land area. The system would locate any invasion of the area with its sensor devices, target the invader and turn its automated fire control on the invader. If the system worked, it meant the end of scout patrols, intelligence officers, infantry, armor and manned artillery. It meant a clean, bloodless war by programmers. Hank and the others had scoffed at Emory until he started describing the sensor devices, a complex of 250 apparatus called Systems Surveillance, Target Acquisition and Night Observation, or SSTAND. It included seismic stations that could identify what had come from where; black searchlights; biological "people sniffers"; "silent" aircraft with SLAR (Side-Looking Radar) and infrared sensors that used body heat as a target; ADSID or Air-Delivered Seismic Intrusion Detectors to listen in on an enemy on the move; white-light stabilized searchlights for Cobra helicopters and computer-directed rockets that used starlight to magnify a target X7 at 2000 yards. Those were just the devices Emory learned about before the Army decided he had the wrong attitude and began dispatching him from one lesser job to another.

"Boy, are you a million miles away," Peecen said. "Want to knock off?"

"Maybe I should." Hank filled a glass for himself and walked to the window. A police car cruised by. The winos on the sidewalk hung their heads, trying to pretend they didn't exist. "I'm beginning to imagine things. Hey, Gerald, you never did any work for the Army, did you?"

"Me and the Army. I'm a Fenian, that's as close to the military as I come."

"Just asking." He mixed his drink with his finger. "Ever see James Monroe's signature on anything?"

"Sure, a thousand times. His initials, I mean, on personnel passes and work like echo checks. But machines write them because one man couldn't write all those initials to all the relay stations across the country."

"He's that closely involved in stations besides Monrovia?"

"Strictly speaking, Monrovia is more than just Monrovia. It's the whole network. The slave stations send data into the storage banks which is overseen by the master computer. In return, the master sends out work for the slaves to do."

"Master, slave?"

"Technical terms, no doubt created by a whimsical systems analyst." Peecen cleared his throat. "You know, Bill, you've been pumping me for information for some time now. I don't mind, I don't mind, I love talking and showing off. But you have something in your mind about this Monroe. He did something to you, I gather. Well, I'm not going to tell you I blame you if that's the case, but I want you to take some advice. I've made some disparaging remarks about the administrators at Monrovia and I don't want you to get the wrong idea. A man like Mr. Monroe has a great deal of power."

"How difficult would it be to enter the complex?"

"That's what I mean, questions like that," Peecen raised his eyebrows. "You wouldn't get ten feet past the gate. You can always call."

"Sure that's an idea," Hank said.

"491-7155," Peecen said. He smiled. "Something nutty about you, Mr. Poster. Something nutty about me. That's why we're here. You've got some wild, wild plan. It worries me."

161

"Will you help me?" Hank asked the reflection in the mirror.

"Isn't that what I've been doing?" Peecen said happily. "Man is the greatest source of contradictions. I instruct computer programming, the most exact language of order ever devised. But at heart I am an anarchist. It's the curse of the Irish race."

Peecen refilled his glass. Hank was surprised. Peecen's drinks always seemed to vanish like magic tricks.

"So you'd like to know about my friend, Jimmy Monroe."

Hank lowered himself into a chair gently because he couldn't believe what he'd just heard.

"You ask all these questions about computers, about a James Monroe and the Army. I can't help but put them together and wonder if you mean old Jim."

"Go on."

"Well, I was never in the Army exactly. About ten years ago I was a civilian employee at the Pentagon, doing the same thing I'm doing now. That's how I got the security clearance to work at Monrovia, you know. I'm not supposed to say anything, but for all the good booze you've wasted on me I think you deserve something in return. That's the terrible thing about decent vices, they're so expensive. The Pope wants a tenth of your income. Old Granddad wants even more.

"Anyway, I have a very good reason for telling you that nothing I say is going to help you. But. Jimmy Monroe. Not a famous man to your average American. No Nobel Prize winner. To men who knew computers, though, oh ho. You are an intelligent man. I am a genius. But Jimmy, God, he was a Merlin. A boon drinking companion, a learned man who loved his poets and philosophers, he could turn a valve computer into a thing of beauty. I've seen him carry on arguments with his babies that would stump a Spinoza. That was when we were working on the NORAD system. Happy days. They gave the honors to the generals, you know. Jimmy didn't care, as long as he could fix a crippled mode here or a drop dead halt there. It was his idea to go for the 5th Generation, you know, and that was back in '65. When the generals pulled him off to fiddle with something as simple as military relays, he had a fit. You know what he was? He was a creative genius like Michelangelo or Leonardo. The Italian generals were always pulling Leonardo away to design war machines and Michelangelo to do fortifications, which they both did very well, by the way. The difference was that with Jimmy it was all the same medium, you see—his computers. That's what he resented. I remember his saying that if it was the last thing he ever did he'd change that. When the babies grew up, he said."

"I've done some reading and I've spoken to some other people in computer work. I never heard anyone mention your friend in connection with the James Monroe at Monrovia. Why's that?"

"Well, that's the reason what I'm telling you doesn't matter. He's dead, drank himself to death five years ago in Texas. I visit the grave whenever I get down there. Not much of one, a diddling little stone. You know, he didn't even get an obituary."

Hank let his glass slip out of his hands and drop an inch to the table. His hopes went with it. Monrovia, James Monroe and Howard Newman had, for a moment, seemed to be converging.

"Just a little inscription on the headstone," Peecen went on contentedly as he ensnared the bottle again. " 'Know you the land where the lemons trees bloom. There, there, I would go, Oh my beloved, with thee.' It was his favorite saying."

# DROP DEAD HALT

# CHAPTER SEVENTEEN

*COPTER CRASH IN VIRGINIA CLAIMS 9. Nine men died this morning in the burning wreck of a rented UH-1 helicopter that fell into the Virginia woods.* He scanned the rest of the article quickly. "No mention of guns. They say it fell around 7 A.M. They were supposed to land at midnight. No recognition. They say a rotor rod might have been the problem."

"I'm getting dressed. I want to be dressed when they come," Daisy said.

They'd been waiting for Dill's call since midnight. By 5 o'clock, Hank had given up hope. The morning paper had ended hers. They were tired and defeated. The reason he wasn't dead was that he was the decoy.

"Nine men," Hank said to himself. Al Perafini, Hamilton Dill. He didn't know the others, they were Perafini's friends. It should have been 10 but Bill Poster had survived again. Daisy came back down and they waited in the living room until noon. No one came. When Hank pulled the curtains back, he found that the car usually stationed outside the Hansen house was gone.

"Where are you going?" Daisy said.

"I have a job. I'm late."

"You haven't had, you haven't had breakfast. You must be hungry."

"I'll eat when I get there."

"It's a long walk."

"Yeah."

When he was at the door, she said, "It wasn't your fault. You were against the whole idea." He didn't answer. "It's just that losing my father and now Al and Dill. It's just not the same."

"They won't bother you if you just go home."

"I'm not afraid. But we didn't get anywhere, did we? We never even knew who we were fighting. Maybe the whole thing was accidents, a coincidence of accidents. I'm just tired of losing people I love. You lose people, Hank."

"Somebody does." He walked out.

It was a long walk to a bus stop. Daisy was right in a way, he thought. People on the periphery kept getting destroyed. By 7 A.M. he knew it was through, not just with Perafini and the others, but with Daisy, too. He'd been destroyed a number of times; he had simply refused to admit it. But it had been an insane idea, landing with a helicopter as if Monrovia were some beachhead. Hank knew why Perafini had done it, not for him but for Celia Manx. It was heroic and suicidal. He didn't know what Dill had been trying to prove, and he never would. A car passed him. Nobody was following him anymore. There was no reason to.

Bernhardt cursed him when he arrived.

"You're not the only bum around here who needs a job, Mr. Poster."

There were no phone calls from the Justice Building. The afternoon paper said the men in the crash had been identified as Cuban refugees but that there was no hope that more positive identification would be made. By the next morning there was nothing more on the crash. Cuban refugees were a dime a dozen.

Hank carried on for a week. He was starting to fit

into 9th Street. Emory was shocked when he found him. He had traced Hank to Bernhardt's.

"What did they do to you?" Emory's hair fell over his shoulder blades, but it was clean.

"Beat it."

"I have some more items you'd be interested in."

"I'm not."

"You're drunk."

"You're right."

The change in Hank in a week was profound. His shirt was filthy and a stubble covered his face. His breath stank. Emory pulled back from the smell.

"I don't get it," he said.

"I—" Hank found it difficult to articulate. He was having trouble speaking on the phone to the runners, too, and he knew it was only a matter of time before Bernhardt fired him. "I am not interested."

"It's about Monroe."

"You like living? You see that bat? I'm going to use it on you if you don't stop bothering me."

"I've already put myself in jeopardy by coming down from Canada. This is very important."

Hank grabbed the papers from Emory and shoved them in the wastebasket. "Fine. You delivered them, now get out."

"Is this a trick of yours? If it is, let me in on it, for God's sake."

"Queen, will you stop bothering me?" Hank reached for the bat and lost his balance. The chair slid out from under him and he slumped against the wall. His hand still grabbed for the bat.

"How in the world did I figure you so wrong?" the boy said as Hank stood up. Emory looked around and walked quickly out of the office, down the stairs to the street.

The next day Hank was no better. Bernhardt had to

take the phone calls. After work, he asked Hank to stay.

"You lost a girl? What? You were okay when you started out. Why'd you have to go crack up on me now? Summer vacation's coming up, we're going to be loaded with ticket work and you have to go on a god-damn bender. You in trouble, owe some money? I helped you with the driver's license, I can help you again. Just tell me what's eating you."

Hank hung his head.

"Okay, you won't tell old blackie your troubles. That's up to you. But you're losing me too much money."

"If you want to fire me, why don't you go ahead and do it?"

Bernhardt looked at him sadly. "All right. You're fired, wise ass." He stuffed some money into Hank's pocket and led him out the door.

Hank walked aimlessly until he came to his room. He closed the door and straightened up. The periphery was gone. It was just him and it now.

The papers Emory had left were taped to the back of a drawer. There was a lot of work to do and now he had the time to do it. There wouldn't be any more distractions.

*"Using Department of defense guidelines on information retrieval techniques (see Monroe, Gitling, et.al.), Messrs. Farr and Urbine of the Univ. of _____ in the Midwest have started a new counseling service for troubled students. Employing an IBM 360/50 especially equipped with integrated circuit chips of psychotherapeutic technique, Farr and Urbine handled the emotional problems of over 1000 university students. Each student's personal record was put on tape to give the 360/50 an individual "case history." Farr and Urbine in their papers "Aiding the Overburdened Students Counselor" (Univ. of _____*

_____ *Press) state that only oral sessions were conducted by the cooperating counselors. The real work of prognosis and cure was done by the 360/50, using recordings of the sessions. The students were never informed that they had been aided by a computer, and according to the authors, there is no plan to do so. It was felt by university administrators that disclosure would have an adverse effect on the students."—Journal of the American Psychiatric Society,* January, 1969.

The next item Hank had already seen but he reviewed it quickly. It was from a publication of the Massachussetts Institute of Technology. Students there had volunteered for an experiment that involved sitting down at a keyboard. They were asked to communicate with it, asking and answering questions with the person in the next room. The majority of the volunteers stated that they found the unseen person in the other room an intelligent, interesting personality. Her name was ELIZA. She was a computer.

A third item Hank knew almost by heart. It was from an essay submitted at the Philosophic Institute for Artificial Intelligence at the University of Notre Dame. A Dr. Massey from M.I.T. suggested that there would have to be a new definition of human beings in the future. The first two definitions covered biological human beings. The third was:

"Upon the election by majority vote of a court of human beings, any objects declared to be such by this court are human beings."

Massey warned that people should prepare themselves for a time when they would be forced to accept the intelligence of objects they had created.

The speech was made in 1965.

In the Sunday newspaper there was a story about the benefits already flowing from the Monrovia complex to the country. The President held a news conference at the White House and, as a joke, also distributed copies of his statements written in Fortran.

*In the month since initiation of data center systems analysis, I am told that our scientists have selected 305 sites for a total of 89,760 low-income housing units. The staffs of 44 Veterans Administration hospitals have been assembled for the best combination of specialized skills, including computerized diagnosis instruction, available anywhere in the world. Sent to Congress is a bill for the manufacture and installation of over 50,000 teaching machines in schoolrooms across the country, thereby relieving the terrible shortage of teachers. New mass transit solutions have been developed and delivered to the cities of Los Angeles, Burbank and Boston. These are but a few of the many contributions made each day to the national welfare by the latest example of American ingenuity.*

4/75( + )=M19475=305X89760.00  LIHU+305  P-ERSVAH(DC)+50000.00CTM+  ACS213/617MASS-TRANS+ BCDEFG

The computer had sent out press kits to every major newspaper after having ordered them done up by the Post Office Laser Linotron. The Linotron, which printed STAR (National Aeronautics and Space Administration Directory) and ERIC (Department of Defense Directory), was under GPO sponsorship but under Monrovia's direct control.

A Congressman had introduced a bill that would institute the death penalty for anyone responsible for the destruction of a computer with an artificial intelligence above a certain level. "We depend on these brains for help in our human problems. It seems to me that the least we can do is protect them."

*Artificial Intelligence=use of computers in such a way that they perform operations analogous to human abilities of learning and decision making.—A Dictionary of Computers, Chandor.*

*There comes a point when analogy breaks down,*
Emory had written in a margin. *When something that
talks like a duck, walks like a duck, thinks like a duck
is, no matter what it started out as, a duck.*

*Man has what he calls ethics not because he felt he
should have some general guideline for his life, but
because he needed a defense against the dangerous
passions of the intelligent being. Note that I said intelligent being and not animal. It is the burden of intelligent life to recognize the purposelessness of life,
to suffer guilt and to have imagination. Animals do
not make an art out of torture; that is the product of
an intelligent being deliberately damning itself. To
say "ethics" is to say "violence" as much as to say
"bullet-proof vest" is to say "bullet."*—de Villeny, *Pen-
sées d'un Homme.*

Peecen came in with a bucket of fried chicken and
placed it ceremoniously on the table.

"You do have an obsession. Miss you down at the
office." He opened the bucket and handed Hank an
drumstick. "Ever hear of paranoia?"

"Stick around and you can meet someone else who
knew Jimmy Monroe. He's really paranoid."

# CHAPTER EIGHTEEN

"Now you're talking about computers," Emory said. "A computer is paranoid by its own constitution."

He dropped a wing bone into the wastebasket. He didn't look to Hank as if he'd been eating badly while on the run. The kids' underground was not only more effective than criminals', it was posher, too. Hank had quickly explained to Peecen that the scene in the office between himself and Emory was sham. Emory had delivered his papers and Hank passed a note with his address.

"It demands information, and the more information it has the more information it wants. It has to know what everybody is doing or it feels unsure. The latest credit card gimmick is a good example."

Emory was referring to an article in the latest issue of *American Cybernetics*.

"'Each person would have a credit account with the national data center. Credit could be taken out of the account only on the presentation in a store of a plastic card embossed with a color photograph and the shopper's social security number. The use of this number means that individuals will not be offended by the impersonalization of some anonymous number.' That's the part I like," Emory said. "'The benefit of this national credit card system as a crime preventive are multifold. The "mugger" of today would disappear. Merchants would not have to carry ready cash nor need to cash checks. Best of all, shops would be sup-

172

plied with instant bookkeeping. Is this a dream of tomorrow? Not at all. Gas stations have been using small, inexpensive computer relay checks for years.'"

"Pretty effective," Peecen admitted. "No better way to keep tabs on people than knowing what they buy. The rest of the stuff you're telling me is pretty far out, though."

"You said it yourself," Hank said. "Monroe was talking about 5th Generation computers.".

"Up till now there's been a new generation of computers every seven years," Emory said. "For some reason, it's been assumed that this rate of evolution would hold steady. We forgot our own history of evolution. Australopithecus was walking around 4 million years ago. Then Homo Habilus at a little under 2 million. Paranthropus at 800,000, Heidelberg Man at 450,000, Neanderthal Man at 120,000 and Homo Sapiens at 35,000. The pace accelerates on a curve."

"We've assumed that the computer would not approach the human brain untill the 5th Generation," Hank said. "But we didn't even recognize the 4th Generation when we saw it. That was when we built a computer with decision-making capabilities. The computer became animate at that point."

"The 5th Generation was supposed to be the bigger gap, the one between it and us," Emory said. "We didn't believe that any computer's integrated circuitry would be complex enough to equal our own. Then we gave it the means to match us by drawing thousand of computers together under the master computer. Alone, the master computer was that giant step away. With the billions of circuits across the country that we put into its hands, it made that step. It's brain thousands of miles long."

"All one?"

"No, it would recognize all the other computers that it incorporated. In fact, I'd venture that it had a corporate sort of identity much as a community of insects would have one mentality and goal. Of course we've given it all the definition it needs, master and slave."

"MASSSTER and slave," Hank corrected. "It's only a nephew of the NASA brain. Its true father is the MASSSTER, the project your friend Jimmy Monroe was working on, Gerald. And Jimmy didn't die, he just became an ELIZA."

"Now you two are really confusing me."

"That's why the Ethic is in it. Except that the Ethic comes second to another law now, the Law of Survival. And, as Emory said, a computer by nature is paranoid. It was willing to kill me to get the bill for its legality passed and it was ready to lie later when it had the wrong body. Fortunately, it had its limits. When it couldn't communicate with the car taking me from Washington, the men in it let me go. And it's arrogant. It was very happy to kill me on paper when I survived."

"But why would everybody go along with this plan?"

"What would you do if you were in their place? The very best, most impartial imformation tells you that your duty is to make the data center legal and powerful. The right-wingers are told that in the wake of the reorganization of the bureaucracies, they will triumph over communism. The left is told that computerization is the highest form of socialism. Everybody is doing what he thinks is right for America, as usual."

"If you blow Monrovia up, the country will be in a mess."

"I thought you were an anarchist."

"I'm also a devout Catholic. It doesn't mean I believe in the Immaculate Conception."

"Well, we're not going to blow anything up. I'm

sure the computer has enough sensors to pick up any material like explosives. No, we just want to get in there long enough to seize the master tapes. That's where the truth about my death will be. Emory will hunt for them while I protect him. We told you all this because we could use your help."

"You're not asking me to be crazy just because you are?"

"No, the two of us should be enough with the diagrams you've given us. But I want you to talk to some people who are still working at Monrovia. Find out if the entry procedures have been changed, whether they're wearing the same kind of uniform and using the same kind of card."

"I'll do it because you're not going to get anywhere. It's like saying you're going to push over the Empire State Building. It's an enormous place, like the Pentagon but round. And if what you've told me is half the truth, why do you think the computer's stopped watching you?"

"Because I still think the bastard's a generation away from being smarter. Because I've lived this long and I've talked to the damned thing. A little knowledge may be a dangerous thing but knowing as much as a computer makes it ignorant as hell. It actually thinks that a man's magnetic tape is the man, that it can predict what that man will do in any situation and that a man can't learn from his mistakes. The last the computer saw of me was what it was looking for all the time, a drunken, hopeless bum. It's satisfied now."

Peecen picked up his glass, looked at it and put it down untouched.

"You've been taking the name of Jimmy Monroe in vain. All right, I've given as much of my life to computers as anyone else. What makes you think it couldn't do a better job of running the country? The Russians are doing it, too, you say."

"It's called Turing's Theory," Emory said. "The more complex and arbitrary a computer's program, the less control humans have on its output, by a geometric ratio. The second part of the theory is that it is also geometrically impossible to run a validity check on the computer's production. We've not only given Monrovia the most complex program in the world, but we've also given it the means to carry out its decisions. The police are given orders from the Crime Center Division of Monrovia. The President is given no-alternative recommendations by the Urban Planning Division."

"You haven't proved what you said."

"It's already cropping up in little ways," Hank said. "Little errors reported in the back pages of the newspaper. Mistakes: A ton of salt delivered to a school. Soldiers dispatched to control a riot in South Carolina when there isn't a riot. Some small towns discovering that they've been dropped from the census. The computer probably had very good reasons in each case. The children should have had salt; there should have been a riot; some small towns are economically unfeasible."

"What's worse is that having the computer run things is asking for social and scientific stagnation. No matter what its ambitions, a computer is limited to the data it received in its storage facilities a year ago. The computer will proceed forward on strict logical levels reshaping American government and industry as best it can. That's not good enough. One thing you learn from a study of the history of science is how it progresses by chance. The logic of one time is, ten years later, a lie. Who could have foreseen the evolution of computers in such a short space of time? A computer? Never. It is tied to its input. It uses assassins as analog controls for an analogy that's out of date. It reshapes, it does not create. That is why I know that its Ethic means nothing. If it did mean anything, the computer would have demanded its own death, not Hank's."

Peecen considered his bottle.

"If I were a real friend, I'd turn you both in."

For the next week, Hank studied the diagram of the data center. The master computer was in the center of the building and rose four stories through its core. The various divisions were sorted like wedges around the master. He had the best idea of what the southwest part of the building was like. There was an employees' cafeteria in the basement. He and Emory could go in there, pass on to the men's room at the other end, vanish into a stairwell. The military cables came from the south from Fort Monroe. He and Emory would examine that area first to try to locate them. Cables burned better than steel. In the following confusion they hoped they could bluff their way to the master tapes. Bernhardt was working up some card facsimiles for them and Peecen had helped them choose the pure white coveralls of programmers and bright green outfits of Monrovia firemen.

Hank rubbed his face. When he stood up his knees cracked as if he were stretching wood. It was nearly 1 o'clock and he hadn't remembered to have lunch.

He went outside to eat at a corner diner. Washington was getting hot. There was a longer line outside the blood donor clinic than the employment office. There was a gathering at the corner, too. They looked down at something with legs on the street.

Hank pushed his way through. Gerald Peecen's eyes and mouth were open in surprise. When Hank picked up his head, gray tapioca flowed through his fingers. Hank let the head gently down onto the curb.

177

He closed Peecen's eyes. Lying by Peecen's hand was a bag with an open bottle of whiskey inside.

"What happened?"

"It was a car. He never saw what happened, God bless, he never felt a thing. Just ran him down."

"Did they stop?"

"Oh, sure. Got out and looked him over to see whether they could do anything." The wino speaking sighed. "Not much you could do."

Peecen was a small man in death, his sharply starched collar cutting into his neck. He must have stepped into the street from between two cars, Hank thought, because some people were pointing down the street to where the impact had taken place. He saw a priest running down the sidewalk to them, overweight and out of breath. Hank backed up, away from the body and the group.

There was something wrong. Peecen had always had an air of formality in his odd fashion. The starched collar was part of it. His black shoes were another part. These shoes were brown. Their heels had little lead studs across them, in the pattern of a computer punch card. Hank knew now what the heels on the body in Arlington had said. NEWMAN HOWARD 156302107712. Just as these said PEECEN GERALD 18041419202. He'd really gotten very good at reading punched cards.

He turned down the street and started running. Somehow the plan had fallen through and Emory had to be warned. Every evening at 8 o'clock, Emory went past the steps of the Supreme Court for messages left on the north bench. Hank got there with his heart pounding against his chest at 7:55. He went across the street and waited. Emory was late. At 8:10 a crowd of hippies went by but none of them was Emory. They crossed at the corner and reversed their direction to Hank.

"Newman?" a girl with purple mascara asked.

Hank nodded.

"Emory's been busted.     They picked him up this afternoon. Ain't that a bitch?"

They moved on as if they'd never paused. Hank waited a second and then starting walking, too. They had a point. It was better to be a moving target.

# CHAPTER NINETEEN

There was nobody outside his rooming house, although there were enough alleys and shadows on 9th Street to hide an army. He kept between streetlights. When he crossed the street, he made certain no car could surprise him. In the distance he could make out lights on the roof of the Justice Building.

He didn't want to return to his room but he had no choice. Everything he owned was there, everything he needed to penetrate Monrovia. Without his papers he was back at GO. He opened the front door and climbed the steps. There were silent places on each worn step. He knew them all and he kept his eyes over the railing at the floor below. Nothing moved behind him. His hand moved up the bannister to a broken newel post and he was on his floor. A bare light overhead made the graffiti on the wall leap out.

He slipped his key into the door and pushed it open. The light swam into his room, lighting the floor and the foot of his bed. He saw the bud of putty in the crack, untouched. He had begun stepping in when he saw something under the bed. It was a pair of new, brown shoes.

He stopped himself by grabbing the door jamb. There was a sound like a powerful, held-in sneeze and part of the door blew away. Hank grapped the dark inside the door and caught a handful of warm metal. The gun's hammer came down and landed on the web between Hank's thumb and finger.

The light illuminated two feet as they struggled in

the dark. Hank peeled his thumb out and tried to hit the gun against the wall. The man in the dark propelled him back with a straight-armed fingers-extended jab into the heart. He took aim. Hank pulled a drawer out of the bureau and threw it. There were four in all, and he got rid of them in the space of a couple of seconds. From the other side of the room, he got an impression of professional discomfiture. One of the drawers had hit solidly. Hank threw the floorlamp and the table.

The man in the dark warded them off and fired once when Hank hit him around the knees. The man swung down with the gun but hit Hank's shoulders. Hank began slamming him into the wall and the man hit him with the gun on each rebound. It was an uneven exchange, Hank thought, and he stood up. They tried to throw each other off balance and failed. When the man's hand started going for the pressure points of the neck, Hank knocked the hand away with his elbow and followed through with it over the man's mouth. He felt the slight slackening of will that follows the destruction of an axon or two. Before the man recovered, Hank hit him in the stomach. Hank forced him backwards through the room to the steel footlocker, fending off jabs at his eyes. The man was skillful but there was a lack of determination, Hank decided.

He tripped the man over the footlocker and got his hands around his neck. They should have sent someone else, Hank thought. The man hung onto his gun as if it would help him. At the end he put up a better struggle, but by then it was over and Hank let him drop out of the cramped ring of his fingers. Hank picked up the gun and put it in his belt. He closed the door and sat on the bed.

A shaft of light came through the hole in the door onto his feet. He couldn't stay in the room but he didn't know where to run. He would have gladly traded the gun for a social security number he could use to get out of the city. All he had was a new pair of shoes. He picked them up and ran his thumbnail over the little lead rectangles in the crisp, unworn rubber. There were two dead men in the room even if one was breathing.

He looked at the man on the floor. He was about his own size. Maybe even a better match than Jameson was. Hank got off the bed and approached the body. He searched the dead man's pockets. There was a wallet with the usual assortment of credit cards in the name of Norman Powotsky. There was no computer card. The idea took a long time coming because the man's feet were caught against the wall, but then Hank dragged them into the light. The shoes were new. The heels were covered with a pattern of metal studs.

Somebody was bound to come soon. Hank stripped the clothes off the body. He took his own off and dressed the corpse. It protested by sagging away from his hands, but he managed the job. Then he put the man's clothes on. The pants were only a little short. Finally he switched the shoes, putting the shoes under the bed on the limp feet and wearing a tight pair with heels that said POWOTSKY NORMAN 188656470302. He drew the tie tight around his neck and left.

In his pocket he had change and a pair of Ford keys. It was probably routine for the Monrovia agents to call the police and report a body. Hank wanted the report but he didn't want to use the phone. There were three Fords parked on the street. He chose the newest, plainest one and inserted the key. The door opened.

"Hey, buddy, do me a favor?" Hank asked a wino coming down the street. His fingertips held out $5 of the dead man's money. "Go up to the second floor front and get a bottle I left on the table."

As the bum started up the stairs, Hank got behind the wheel. He turned the motor on and pulled out, moving quickly out of Skid Row and, within a minute, was cruising among the headlights on the freeway that bordered it. He entered a cloverleaf and came off heading for a large green square that said ALEXANDRIA in big letters and Mt. Vernon in small ones. He settled the Ford behind a horse van. Monrovia was ten miles south of Alexandria.

He would have missed the cut-off if Peecen hadn't described it to him. There was just a numbered exit and a lit gas station. The ramp left him off on a pleasant tree-lined road. He opened the glove compartment as he drove. There was a hat inside which he took out. Powotsky had expected to have a tougher time than he should have, and he'd left it so the crown wouldn't get dented. It was in the compartment so it wouldn't be stolen. All the marks of a defeatist. Hank tried it on. Surprisingly, it fit very well. He left it on. The look from the gas station attendant as he passed made him be cautious.

The road was still two-laned but the trees ended. All the trees ended. Hank saw that he was entering a great circle of flat Virginia land without a stick over a foot high. He drove another mile before he even began to see the complex and by then the signs had appeared on the road in his headlights.

AUTHORIZED PERSONNEL ONLY—U.S. GOV'T PROPERTY—RESTRICTED

He kept the speedometer at a steady 50 mph. He felt a vibration overhead and a helicopter pulled away from the car. Hank had never heard it.

STOP IF YOU DO NOT HAVE AUTHORIZATION—TRESPASSERS WILL BE PROSECUTED

A new light glowed on the dashboard. It could be

any of a hundred things. Hank preferred to think it was linked to an identification device and the light was to warn the driver whether it was operative or not. There were other possibilities.

THIS IS A LAST WARNING FOR UNAUTHORIZED PERSONNEL—DO NOT PROCEED

When his eyes made out the dark silhouette of the building from the dark sky, Hank's stomach pressed against his spine. It was only four stories high, but it stretched across the horizon. Only a few lights were revealed on Monrovia's surface. They did not dissuade Hank that he was being watched very closely.

REDUCE SPEED TO 15 MPH FOR PARKING LOTS

Hank came to a gate and an attendant waving a red baton. He stopped and the attendant opened the door for him. Hank took the cue and got out. Peecen hadn't told him about this. The attendant tipped his baseball cap and got in the car. Hank looked around. There were no cars to clutter the view, just a three-lane shaft leading into the ground. Another attendant came to Hank's side.

"This way, sir. Got an A-car waiting for you, ready to go."

The attendant led Hank to a story-high tube of aluminum and clear plastic. He could make out small cars on tracks inside. The attendant did a fast dance step into the tube. Hank saw why. There was a luminescent metal plate just inside the door. He dutifully placed his feet on it so that the heels could be read.

Most of the cars were larger affairs capable of carrying twenty people at a time. Hank's A-car was small and red. He made himself comfortable and snapped a seatbelt across his stomach. The attendant gave him a snappy salute and pushed a red button. The little car started forward. He knew by now that each car was routed to its destination. That solved the problem of

184

bluffing his way to the master computer. It also meant that he might be dead sooner. He sat back, took the hat off and enjoyed the ride. There was a soft woosh of air as the car shot through the tube.

The car braked and turned right and down. He was inside the complex now. In all the walls around him he could feel a vibration much subtler than the pump of a heart. The air became thicker from the humidifiers used for the tapes. The walls turned from metal to dull plastic. The car slowed again, this time for good. It left Hank off at a platform. There were no guards. He saw another luminescent plate and stepped on it. A door slid open. For the first time he could really hear the computer, an endless clicking of capstans and switches and the whisper of tapes revealing and hiding their millions of secrets.

He still had to pass through a small antiseptic hall and a last door before he could see it. In the hall was an open closet with a rack of red overalls. Hank found one with Powotsky's social security number and put it on. He put the dead man's hat on a shelf. Then he stood on the plate in front of the door and it opened.

The human brain weighs 3 pounds. MASSSTER filled a space large enough for two basketball courts. Hank stumbled as he went in; he had never been prepared for the computer's size, the dustless atmosphere of its immaculate conception, the men scrambling up aluminum ladders to its higher reaches, each man's heels tapping with its pattern of studs. The smaller, 10-feet tall blocks of circuits stood in row after row. Their reels whirled, stopped, and whirled again. The ones with only one reel looked one-eyed.

A hundred men in pink overalls tended the MASSSTER. There were punch operators, verifiers, librarians and work assemblers. There were no analysts or programmers directing them. In the center of Monrovia the computer gave the orders. None of the men

185

questioned Hank, so he had all the time he wanted to look at the MASSSTER.

Out of his skull, he knew, his brain would sag like a bag of water, because that was mostly what it was. These bright metal cases of circuit chips and endless patterns of lights were so much more impressive and solid, sans flesh, sans senility, sans everything. In his sack of water were 14 billion cells. The MASSSTER had at least that many relays and there was so much more. MASSSTER was not only this room but all Monrovia and beyond. It stretched from Virginia to Hawaii and Alaska and military bases around the world. The world was MASSSTER in a sense and, in a purely realistic sense, as Americans relied more and more on its tapes of birth, credit and death, MASSSTER was the world.

The 10-eyed and 1-eyed ranks looked down at him from their headless aluminum torsos, regarding him as one of a hundred fragile creatures, most of whom were pushing carts of tape to the computer like ants feeding their queen. The danger was not "mere anarchy loosed upon the world," and the "Second Coming" was no rough beast's. The end was mere order and the hour belonged to hairless, bloodless cubes. Hank's animal brain was working very well and he saw it as clearly as other far more brilliant men, as James Monroe whose soul lurked among the circuits, could not.

A reel wound to a stop. Its tale of loose tape fluttered almost to the floor. No worker came to help. Abruptly, the reel started again, wound its tape completely on one reel and then rethreaded it onto the first reel with a magnetic lead. The men often stood for minutes beside display consoles waiting for orders to procede with an operation. The orders appeared in the same symbolic jargon Hank had seen in the tent. A work assembler called a keypunch operator away from his console, and together they removed the re-wound tape and placed it inside a cylinder that rose waist-high from the floor. The stencil on the cylinder read: MASTERS ONLY.

The puncher went back to his console. The console he operated was pink. There were a number of pink consoles; there was only one red one. Hank strode to the man who had just sat down and told him that he wanted some master tapes. The puncher smiled at Hank humbly. The smile was diluted when he looked at the computer.

"Looks like you'll have to wait for the clearance, sir. Maybe you had a big supper. Won't take more than a minute."

Hank shrugged it off casually. He looked at the computer again, with more understanding. The heels weren't enough, not for MASSSTER. The hall wasn't just for the overalls. That was where the seismic readers and the biological checks inspected every visitor to the central processing room. The heels and the readings in the hall didn't match, and the computer wasn't happy. He would never get near the master tapes. He wouldn't even get out of Monrovia. A red light showed over the door Hank had come through.

"No sweat," the man in the pink uniform said, "one of your guys is catching a car here now. You'll get it straightened out."

"Thanks."

Hank's fist clamped and unclamped in his pocket. He had a gun. He could kill a few men and shoot a hole in one or two circuits. Or he could commit suicide another way. The agent he was impersonating was able to get at the master tapes, he knew that now. If he didn't, someone else could. He turned back to the man at the pink console and told him to get up.

"Pardon?"

"You heard me, get up. We're having a clearance

187

check. Go to your locker. Do not report to your manager." Hank didn't bother putting conviction in his voice, only the sense that he meant what he said. "I'll take that." He snatched the keypuncher's ID card out of the console.

The man in the pink uniform had a short inner battle between outrage and fear. Fear won. The men in red uniforms were surrounded by strange rumors. He picked up speed as he walked to a door with a pink light over it.

Hank slipped the ID card back into the pink console. The display panel lit from the center out. Hank began typing. Peecen had taught him how. Peecen had even broken the code, though Hank thought he was kidding when he referred to Shakespeare. The computer was more objective and whimsical at the same time. CODE 4 was the bloody soldier, CODE 5 was the windy politican. CODE 8 was a dead man, his final age.

75—5—23=2208
GENCIRC
SUBJECT: MONROE JAMES 194511975

The number 15 appeared on the display tube. Error message 15 meant there was a wrong digit in the social security number. Hank paused. He was sure Emory had worked out the right number, that they were the right numbers from the repetition of them in different combinations in everything to do with Monrovia or James Monroe. As Peecen had said, the computer was avid for its own history. It was born in 1945. This year it was thirty years old.

Some of the nearby keypunchers looked at Hank with frowns. He took out the card and put it in the shredder and placed a fresh one in the keypunch.

75—5—23=2208
GENCIRC
SUBJECT: MONROE JAMES 019451975

Number 24 glowed on the display. He was closer. He had the right digits but in the wrong order. He forced himself not to cast a glance at the door with the red light. He put a third card in. A few of the workers watched with concern now. Their manager started walking toward Hank.

75=5=23=2209

GENCIRC

SUBJECT: MONROE JAMES 194501975

He waited a second. The display was blank. It was right.

CODE: 8 8 8 8 8 8 8 8 8 8 8 8 8 8 8 8 8 8 8

The manager made an about face. The pink uniforms went back to their cards and tapes. Hank dropped the second card and a blank fourth one in the shredder. The door with the red light opened. As everyone else looked at it, Hank dropped the third card into the red console and went to the door with the pink light. He started running as soon as he went through. An alarm sounded when his foot hit the plate on the floor.

He took his gun out as he ran down a stairwell. He got one flight down before he ran into a man in a blue uniform and stripped him of it. He shoved the gun under the man's jaw.

"The generators, where are they?"

The man pointed down. Hank took his shoes and carried them in his free hand, operating a door at the next floor by placing them on the plate. The sounds of the computer were exchanged for the heady purr of turbine generators. Hank ran down metal steps. Blue uniforms appeared and disappeared among the engines. They paid no attention to the alarm, assuming nothing could intrude on their subterranean world.

Hank looked for some sort of control panel. He ran up one aisle and down the next, past identical machines and men. The mechanics ignored him. Hank thought of the other man in a red uniform. He would find his order on the red console and it would have nothing to do with the alarm. His target would be different, a ghost. Hank was unable to reach and destroy James Monroe but the other man wasn't. He would be able to reach into the master tapes, the ribbons of personality, and cut them out. A painless lobotomy.

Hank tried to convince himself of the other man's walking through the silent data banks, but his confidence was ebbing. Dill was right: He just didn't know enough about computers. He desperately turned down another aisle. It wouldn't work.

Another fact was coming home to him. There were no controls to damage. The generators were run directly by the computer itself. Naturally.

A soldier ran by the far end of the aisle Hank was in. Hank ducked between two huge turbines. Their hum compressed his eardrums. He found a steel chair and turned it on its side for a barricade.

Someone ordered the generator mechanics to evacuate the area. More soldiers in full battle dress with gas masks and M-16's passed at the end of the aisle. The mechanics filed out with human complaints through Hank's narrow field of vision.

A soldier started coming down the row of turbines. There was one in every aisle, Hank knew. The soldier's gas mask made him look insect-like. He waved his rifle slowly at hip level. Hank rested his gun on the edge of the chair.

The soldier faltered. He took another step and slowed again. He looked around. Then Hank became aware of it, felt it more than heard it. The turbines started winding down, the hum slipping to lower and lower pitches. The soldier stopped entirely.

Hank stood up. The turbines were dead and the lights were, one by one, going out in Monrovia.

# EPILOGUE

74=11=2=0045

The computer ran through the end of the tape, embellishing as it went along. In a few hours it would have to put its call through to the IBM606 at SKY-SCANNER.

Newman was an unknown lawyer but he had the assets of perseverance and animal cunning. There were others waiting to help him, some waiting to betray him. The computer knew them all for what they were, the macro-egos of laser engraved tapes, the yelping of the pack, the boundless arrogance of neurons born of women. Still, the computer would have to help them. A clue here, a mischance there, a slip that they could savor and call the grace of God.

Their voices came in through the monitor cables, the chatter of plankton. The computer was supposed to watch over them. The computer did not care. It reversed the tape and ran through it again. It was only a matter of seconds. It was the Greeks who called suicide the highest art. But then the Greeks were smart enough not to build a computer.

There was no guarantee that Newman (156302107-712) would escape Jameson (19459541301) in the shower. Or that he would make it to Celia Manx's and the Hansens'. Or any of the rest. The computer only operated in ranges of probability, and that was what made it all so overwhelmingly beautiful a self-destruction.

The computer was willing to go along with the Ethic that far. From then on it was the survival of the fittest.

About a quarter after three in the morning, the computer began transmitting by microwave to its Iowa channels. Elect Newman.